Coaling Station A
The Rise and Fall
of an Oil Boomtown!

Dear Brittani

Thank you to
being so awesome!

enjoy the Adventure!

Coaling Station A
The Rise and Fall
of an Oil Boomtown!

by Duncan McCollum

Aptos, California

February 2018

This is a work of fiction based on historical fact. Because history is written and rewritten at different times and with different purposes, it is impractical to warrant that all of the information in this book purported to be so will meet critical standards for accuracy, but assuredly the author's purpose is to convey an interesting story about the people and the time and way they lived.

Coaling Station A
The Rise and Fall
of an Oil Boomtown!

Published by Seton Publishing

ISBN-13: 978-1981544219
ISBN-10: 1981544216

Printed in the United States of America

Table of Contents

Publisher's Note

This is the second of Duncan McCollum's series of historical novels about California before the day of the locusts, the film industry, and SillyCon Valley. His first book, *The Adventures of Little Big Jim,* was primarily set in the mid/late 19th century and told of a boy becoming a man through a series of incredible adventures.

Now with *Coaling Station A*, Duncan weaves a gritty and poignant tale of the early lawless days of the early 1900s during California's second gold rush, that for *black gold*. The story takes place in the lower end of the Central Valley where the oil boom came in with a gush. Actually many gushers of billions of barrels of the stuff.

The roughnecks and the corrupt power elite who pulled their strings were a dangerous force facing the good folks of the region. The sheriff was in big money's pocket, but not the newspaper, whose editor and top reporter struggled valiantly to restore some sense of law and order, and moral justice. Yes, it's an exciting, action-packed tale that will keep your pages turning.

Tony Seton
Carmel, California

Dedication

This book is lovingly dedicated to my grandfather Fay
James McCollum and his bairn. Born in Salinas in 1883,
Mac lived a colorful life filled with adventure, music and
... fishing.

One day, circa 1970, while I was walking with him
somewhere in a Coalinga neighborhood, he stopped and
looked up at an airplane as it flew overhead. He paused
then looked at me and said, "Dunc, I've lived to see the
buggy whip traded in for a Model A, I eagerly read about
the Wright Brother's first flight, and I recently watched
as man took his first steps on the moon."

Another time, while heading to the Sierra for a
backpacking trip, I thought to stop in Coalinga and visit
Mac. This was somewhere around 1978 making him
about 95. I became worried when he didn't answer his
phone. When I finally arrived at his house on California
Street, I found him slumped over on a bench under the
shade of an old cottonwood tree. He was dressed in
khaki pants and a muscleman T-shirt. It must have been
105 degrees in the shade. When I woke him, Mac looked
up at the old push lawn mower he'd apparently been
wrestling around the rather large lot all morning and

said, "Son, if I ever live to be 95 again, I'll not buy a house on a corner lot!" Mac passed away in 1980, he was 97 years old.

I would also make special mention of his wife, Belle. Though I never knew her, I certainly knew of her. She was the glue that created such a loving yet rowdy and talented family. Of their bairn, Aunt Kristi lived to be 98, Aunt Betty 98, my Uncle John 93, and my incredible and loving father, A. James McCollum ll, lived to be 91.

This book is also dedicated to all of Mac and Belle's descendants, known as the Coalinga branch of the Clan McCollum.

Prelude

One of my fondest memories was listening to my grandfather F. J. "Mac" McCollum spinning yarns of the old days. These were usually told in some odd dialect such as Yiddish, broken German or Italian-American, Gaelic, or some other tongue he'd mastered during his acting days in vaudeville. He met my grandmother during a stint of "light opera" sometime around 1907-1908. Mac, Belle, his wife, and all four of their kids were very musical and spent most nights gathered around the family piano singing the old vaudeville tunes I grew up listening to. I am very fortunate to have many of those charts in my possession today, such as *Music Vots Music Must Come From Berlin, Oy Katinka, Heinie Waltzed Round on His Hickory Limb*, and my favorite, *My Cousin Caruso*.

One of my favorite stories was Mac's poem entitled *The Row Laid Low*, which is found in this volume. It memorializes Coalinga's Whiskey Row and its colorful albeit dark history. *The Row Laid Low* depicted the fire that destroyed Fifth Street's Whiskey Row in 1915. This is the story that brought *The Lady Known As Lou* to life.

Grandpa Mac arrived in Coalinga in 1910 as a reporter for the *Coalinga Record* that he eventually purchased, and acted as its editor, even as he was well into his 80s. His column was called *The Fifth Street Philosopher* and his pen name was "Joe King". Whether this was his sense of humor or the fact that Coalinga resided in Kings County, I'll never know.

He has stated elsewhere that in his first seven days on the job in a rough boom town, there were three shootings and one heavyweight prize fight to report on.

Several of the stories in *Coaling Station A* are based on actual events my grandfather told me about. Including the fateful "fishing trip" event when a local thug tried to convince Mac to stop writing stories about certain unsavory citizens of the county. This was when Mac, while driving, pulled the Colt .38 he had hung from the wheel of his Model A and shot a jackrabbit through the haunches as it zigged and zagged speedily – although not fast enough – across the desert.

Mac had left San Francisco on a clipper ship bound for Alaska three days before the earthquake of 1906. There was no ship-to-shore back then, so this landlubber had no idea about the rough seas they would encounter on their way to Ketchikan, Alaska. He bought the Colt .38 revolver while in Alaska that same year. It still resides with the family to this day.

Dry-Hole Charlie was a real person whose reputation is explained in his name.

Old Pete, the horse who pulled the wagon at the beginning of the story is the namesake of the horse my great-great grandfather James McDougall owned when he served as the first marshal of Salinas. He'd attach Old

Pete to a wagon and throw drunks in it when they became too unruly or just plain passed out. He'd tell Old Pete to take them to jail. When McDougall got done making his rounds, Old Pete would be waiting in front of the jailhouse with his prisoners passed out in the wagon. When McDougall was shot in the lung while trying to stop a gun fight between two of Salinas's citizens, he was taken to Tassajara Hot Springs to recover. He died at 84 years old due to pneumonia he eventually contracted from the lead bullet still in his lung.

The following are some excerpts taken from an old manuscript I found while going through my father's papers. Entitled "The History of Coalinga," they are from a radio broadcast in 1967 presented by United States Savings Bonds and Radio Station KOLI Coalinga.

> – In its earliest history the whole area was under water. Geologists and rock collectors have found a wealth of fossils. The mountains surrounding Coalinga are covered with sand dollars, scallop shells, sharks' teeth, leaf impressions, and many other fossil forms. Mammal fossils have also been found. A mastodon, a camel, and two species of ancient deer have also been found.

> – It is uncertain when the first man wandered into the region. Mortars, arrowheads, beads, a few bones and skulls as well as various other artifacts have been discovered there. There was known to be an Indian village near Poso Chana which possessed the only real drinkable water in the region. *Poso* is the Spanish name for well and

Chana was the name of a Yokut Indian chief. The coastal Indians would travel over the mountains to trade with the local Yokut Indians of the San Joaquin Valley at Poso Chana. They would trade dried fish and shells for dried tule roots, grass nuts, seeds, baskets, and oil contained in baskets woven in the shape of bottles.

– In the 1840s a Spanish-Mexican family, the Hicuerras, came to the Coso Chana and chased the Indians away. Following the Higuerras, came several Spanish-Mexican families, who settled the Poso Chana, Jacalitos and Los Gatos canyons. They were engaged in stock raising.

– It was during this time that some of California's notorious bandits had their hideouts in the nearby hills. Joaquin Marietta's gang often used the Joaquin Rocks. This was near Cantus Creek where he and the original Three-Finger Jack were Killed. Tiburcio Vasquez was another well-known bandit of the area. He was eventually captured and publicly hung in San Jose.

– In 1887, the Southern Pacific railroad extended its line into Warthog canyon south of Coalinga. This was to service the abundant coal mines in the area. The Railroad built three switching stations. These were called Coaling Station A, B and C, hence the origin of the name of the California city, Coalinga.

– As early as 1865, the oil seepage nine miles north of Coalinga attracted some attention.

When men appeared on the streets of Millerton, the original seat of Fresno County, trying to sell oil in gallon cans, many became interested in the barren and desolate landscape that would become one of the richest oil strikes in history. In 1890, the first well was brought in. It produced 10 barrels of oil a day from a depth of 135 feet. A windmill pump was used to raise the oil to the surface. Work continued and in 1896, Chandler and Canfield brought in a well that flowed 300 barrels a day. This well was 890 feet deep. More people were attracted and by 1898 there was a settlement, in Oil City, of 24 houses and 40 people. It boasted to be the richest town, per capita, in the valley. An estimated 30 "dry" holes were drilled at Oil City at the average cost of $25,000 per well. Looking for oil wasn't cheap. The oil was there, however, and the boom was on.

Many of the wells made oilfield history. Some of these famous wells were: Confidence#2, Souer Dough #3, Lucile #1, the Famed Blue Goose, and the Silver Tip which produced 36,000 barrels of oil in one 72-hour period. Phoebe Hearst, mother of publisher, William Randolph Hearst bought the lease on Blue Goose. The Blue Goose and other wells mentioned had produced over one million barrels of oil each. In 1910, the oilfields were producing 44,000 barrels daily, from 590 wells. This brought the revenue of nearly $30,000 daily and over $10 million a year, which was serious money back then. At the time of this radio broadcast of 1967, Coalinga had produced over one billion barrels of oil. This makes Coalinga one of the largest oil producers in the United States.

> – In 1915 a fire destroyed Whiskey Row which was rebuilt, but was never the same. A sister town called Circle City, which was just across the tracks, burned two years later, leaving homeless the over 300 ladies of the night who resided there. The more civilized citizens of the once wild and woolly town, took a stand and ran the remaining riffraff out of town. And much to the great surprise of everyone in Fresno County, they declared Coalinga a "Dry City" in 1919.

Today you may be familiar with the large cattle yards of Harris Ranch you can see while traveling along Interstate Highway 5 in California's Central Valley between San Francisco and Los Angeles. This is the turnoff to the once booming economy and boomtown of the now sleepy and almost forgotten town of Coalinga.

<u>*Coaling Station A*</u>

It was early June 1888, and Pa was on duty at the coaling station awaiting the Number 3. She was a Southern Pacific Steam Engine carrying passengers to and from Los Angeles and San Francisco as well as stops in between. She also hauled a slew of boxcars that were typically filled with coal, cattle, timber, cotton, wool, or some other marketable goods. She would arrive at 7:35 AM and took a 30-minute stop at the station before heading on up the track toward her destination.

Pa was both the telegrapher and switchman for the Coaling Station A train depot, one of the three coaling stations being established by the Southern Pacific Railroad to haul out the coal dug out of nearby mines. He'd often tell me how important it was for him to keep track of all the trains comin' and goin' up and down the line. This was not an easy job, because there were no established time zones across the States back in those days. Every town was still setting their local clocks according to "high noon"; that was whenever the sun was directly over their own town. Through the use of the telegraph and something called Morse Code, Pa was able to determine where the trains were and when to expect them to arrive.

Sometimes there'd be trains comin' and goin' both ways at the same time and he'd have to decide which train to let through first and which train to switch onto a sidetrack. Sometimes if I was with him he'd let me pull the switch, which diverted the trains. It was a big responsibility, and I was always nervous about getting it right. There were too many stories of trains colliding, usually because the telegrapher was sleeping on the job or he just plain missed the mark. Ma said Pa would get all wore out with all that thinkin' he had to do, and so I'd try not to bother him much when he come home.

Another part of his job was to meet the train when it pulled into the depot and inspect the boxcars while the train crew loaded coal and took on water. He'd always have fresh brewed coffee ready for the crew, and when they'd finished the loading, they'd come inside and have a cup before headin' on up the line. Oftentimes Ma would send him with a basket of buttermilk biscuits and fresh churned butter for the crew. One of the engineers once told me that Pa's coffee was strong enough that you could float a horseshoe on it. I remember trying this once. I couldn't make it float but we drank the coffee anyway.

Pa would tell me about the hobos, or freeloaders as he

would call them, who used to climb into an unlocked boxcar and ride the rails. He'd say they would be hitching a ride from "who knows where to somewhere else." Pa never bothered them much. He felt bad for the fellas and would oftentimes even share the little food Ma gave him for lunch. Ma said his heart was too big, and often got in the way of his judgment.

There were a few ranches in the area, but water was scarce and most what there was of it wasn't drinkable. We lived on a little farm outside of a town called Huron, which was about 30 miles southeast of the station. Pa would hitch our only horse, Old Pete, to the buggy and head to work every morning about 3:30 AM. Ma would always be up in time to feed him breakfast and make him a box lunch. Pa said he liked to get up early; no one to trouble his thinking so he could consider the troubles of the world. Whenever I asked him what he was considering, he'd never tell me, he'd just say that he done figured it out and was now thinking on to the next problem.

On one particular morning, Pa was almost to the station when he was stopped by a man on horseback, who was blocking his passage. The man pulled out a six shooter and told Pa to get off the buggy. Pa never had much back-up in him, and when he refused, the man just plain shot him. Pa was found a few hours later by the evening watch. When Pa didn't show up at the depot, Jennings, who was the night shift telegrapher, figured Pa was running late and so just started heading for home.

Lucky it was, because whoever had shot Pa was a pour aim. The bullet tore through Pa's left shoulder, missing his heart by a half-inch but nicked his left lung on its way out. Jennings came across Pa wandering in the dark, said Pa was talkin' nonsense still trying to make it to work. Jennings was able to plug the hole and get Pa to Doc Leeper's home in time to save his life. Jennings had fought for the South in the war between the states and had become pretty good at plugging up bullet holes.

Old Pete made it home the next day, but minus the buggy. He still had the rigging attached, but the leather had been broken. Pa said he'd been meaning to repair the old rigging, but never got around to it. It was lucky for Old Pete that he hadn't, and for us too. The buggy was located a week later by chance. There was an old sheepherder in the Kettleman Hills name of Pedro Da Soto. He was moving his flock up toward Priest Valley when he ran across the wreckage. The sheriff said the buggy was found at the bottom of a canyon. He also said there were a few barrels in the wreckage. It looked like they had been filled with somethin' called oil.

Black Bart was a local bandit in the area, who'd been robbing stage coaches lately and was said to be the likely suspect. Pa said it wasn't him though. It was said that Black Bart had never fired a shot in any of the holdups he was credited for, and he usually only wanted Wells Fargo money. Nevertheless, the local paper blamed it on Bart and Pa became a local celebrity for a time. Pa never recovered fully, and eventually contracted pneumonia in his left lung. We buried him in the fall of '05. He was 50 years old.

My name is Alexander McCoy; I'm the only child of Clara and William McCoy. I was born on July 2nd 1885. I'd been working as a reporter for the local newspaper for almost ten years when I finally got the break I was looking for.

Fifth Street

I was investigating the latest murder that took place on Fifth Street in a little town called Coalinga. Fifth Street was better known as Whisky Row. There'd been a lot of roughnecks turning up dead lately and the townsfolk were beginnin' to get concerned. I'd been nosin' around a few joints along the Row, when I was approached by an aging prostitute. Her name was Lou, and she'd been in town since the beginning of time. Oil had been discovered seeping out of the surrounding desert as early as 1865, but hadn't really been considered substantial until somewhere around 1888, this was a couple months after my Pa had been shot. Even though the shooter was never found, Pa had a suspicion of who the man was, but he'd never let it be known.

Raymond Hicks had a big spread up in Priest Valley. He had driven several hundred head of cattle up there a few years back and just settled in. Pa said the brands were a mixed lot, and that he wondered how many local ranches were missing a few head in the wake of Hick's passing. What bothered him even more was how Hicks had somehow taken the notion to purchase much of the land surrounding Coaling Station A, even before the discovery of oil was made public. When Hicks was asked about it, he attributed his real estate aspirations to mere luck.

Lou asked me to meet her at the Riggins, a popular saloon among the Fifth Street inhabitants. I agreed to meet her later that day, around 6:30, as I wanted to be as inconspicuous as possible. This was when the bar would be filled up with roughnecks just getting off their shift. That's what we called the oil workers. They were a dangerous, unsavory lot who loved to fight as much as they loved their oil. Fifth Street had a reputation which I wanted no part of.

Let me tell you about Fifth Street. It was the harder part of town, better known as Whiskey Row. There are many a story that can be told about the goings on there. I will fill you in a bit along the way. It is said that on any given night more than 4,000 men would frequent the some 250 saloons and 35 to 50 whorehouses. There was at least one killing a night, but sometimes three or four. Sheriff Murray didn't bother investigating these anymore, because nobody ever saw anything, or if they did, they had tight lips and kept it to themselves.

With the discovery of oil, the town sprang up in a few weeks. It was as though someone just rolled out a carpet and a town jumped up. When someone started asking what the town should be called, Jack Anderson looked confused saying the town already had a name, Coalinga. He simply misread the sign on the road into town. He mistook the sign that said Coaling A as one word... Coalinga. So the town was named. The new town mayor was John Adams and he liked it, so it stuck.

When Lou appeared, she was all made up in an attempt to resemble the lady she had once been. Only now everything that could had sagged. Her face resembled that of a made-up doll, pasty white with painted-on rosy cheeks, while her red lipstick overshot its natural borders. Her dress was full of ruffles, attempting to accent the curves of her younger self, while her brassiere vainly attempted to hold up what was left of her once ample bosom. She still carried herself with pride though, as she navigated her way through the crowd to the table I occupied, which was in the darkest corner of the saloon I could find.

"Hello, Alex," she opened. "I'm grateful you would meet with me. I have some information that I have kept to myself for far too long. Let me start by saying I know who the man is who shot your father that night, so many years ago. He's still alive and I now fear your life may be in danger. What I'm about to tell you could get us both killed, but I can keep the secret no longer. What they have said about old man Hicks is true, he was always a very dangerous and powerful man. Then when his young nephew, Darwin, and his sidekick, Jack Reynolds, arrived on the scene some years back, Hicks realized a renaissance. He was getting older and was losing his foothold, but those two have been able to secretly carry forward what Hicks has had planned for the valley all these past years. They have been the men responsible for many of the killings both now and in the past."

I was aware of the fact that Darwin Anthony acted as his uncle's foreman, apparently running the ranch operations. Jack Reynolds had the nickname of Three-Finger Jack. He was named after the California outlaw who was killed in 1853 along with Joaquin Murrieta. Murrieta and Jack were notorious bandits who robbed unsuspecting miners of their gold as well as holding up stagecoaches laden with the spoils of the gold fields. Young Reynolds had lost the little finger of his right hand in an accident along the San Francisco waterfront when he was just a kid. When Raymond Hicks first met young Reynolds years ago, he noticed the deficit and immediately pinned him with the handle. It was believed Reynolds enjoyed the nickname, and was proud to be associated with the famous bandit.

This interesting note, when Murrieta and the real Three-Finger Jack were killed back in '53, the governor of California was offering a $1,000 reward for each. So their assailants cut off Three-Finger Jack's hand as well as Murrieta's head to verify their success and to collect the reward. Jack's hand and Murrieta's head were placed in glass jars full of alcohol then displayed in various cities and towns around the state. They were great crowd pleasers and people would flock to the exhibits paying the $1 admittance fee to view them.

When I was ten years old, my pa and I rode up to an old mining town called Murphys to see the display. Although I did get sick to my stomach, I was very happy to have seen them. I believe this is one of the things that lead me into the field of journalism. Later accounts of the slaying disputed Murrieta's death and it is said that his sister was overheard to say Murrieta was alive and well living in Chile. Jack's hand and the would-be Murrieta's head were on display in San Francisco when the earthquake of '06 struck and they were lost for all time.

Wanting to order a drink for Lou and me, I flagged down a waitress. I was hoping to keep her tongue loose before she had second thoughts and froze up. She ordered her whiskey straight, so I decided I better purchase a bottle. She waited for the bottle and I didn't push her to speak, wanting to allow her to control the conversation. I was afraid if I got too pushy she'd clam up. Besides she had sought me out, this was her story to tell. She poured herself a shot and then another. Next, she pulled out the makings and rolled herself a smoke. I was beginning to enjoy the encounter, dangerous as it was. Lou was quite a gal. I held out a match for her. She took a long draw letting the smoke roll out of her nose and mouth. Then she looked at me through her false eyelashes and blood-shot eyes.

The Cover-up

"Hicks has been a customer of mine for a long time," she started. "He'd get whiskey'd up and come a-courtin', or so he called it. One night several years ago when he'd come a-lookin' for me, he was all broke up. Said he'd had an accident. Said his buggy hit a rut in the road and went appetite over tin-cup down a gully. He wanted me to patch him up, said the doc was too far to go and that he had trouble even making it to my place. I was young then and hadn't really chosen my profession yet, but I was already popular with the fellas.

Anyways, I done cleaned him up. He had broke a couple ribs, but was mostly dirt-covered, bruised, and scratched. One thing I didn't think about at the time was the greasy stuff that was all over him. But now I know'd it was oil that covered 'im. Wasn't much of that stuff around back then, it was before the boom, so I didn't rightly know 'bout what it was and so paid it no mind. Fact is, the discovery came about 2 or 3 months after Hicks visited me that night. One thing though, as he was leaving he told me, it would be good for my health if I kept this evening's events to myself. I did, and this is the first I've spoke of it since. One thing I know'd about Hicks, even back then, was I wern't wanting to get on his bad side."

Lou paused, taking a long draw off her smoke. Wondering if she was questioning how much she should tell me, I took the opportunity to pour her another shot and one for myself. I asked if she was hungry and she said she could eat. The waitress was close by so I beckoned her over.

"What will ya have?" she asked me. I ordered a steak and potato. "The usual for you Lou?" she asked and Lou nodded yes.

Lou sat there looking into her glass so I ventured a question. "What makes you think my life is in danger? What is it that has you worried?"

"I ain't worried, but I'd miss your articles if you ended up dead. I've followed you ever since you started writing for *The Record*, and have taken a liking to your style. You're fair and honest," she said.

"That's the way journalism is supposed to be," I replied.

"Ain't the way I see it," she insisted. "Seems to me most stories these days have the flavor of the oil companies and the people who represent it.

"I been around a long time, Alex, and I know'd a

thing or two." Lou paused again. Nursing her stogie back to health, she seemed to be lost in her own world. Then she continued. "There's a stretch of land up on Kettleman Hills owned by old man Walker. Seems he don't want to sell. Problem is, Hicks want to buy.

"Hicks was over the other night – oh, he ain't a-cour- tin' me no more, he just likes to hear himself talk and use me for a sounding board. Since I never said no- thin' about that buggy wreck he thinks I'm a safe bet. Only trouble is, I'm getting tired of holding all this stuff in my head. Can't seem to drink enough whisky to keep my head silent no more. It was easier when I was younger, the boys kept me so busy I never had time to think. Now I'm old and practically out to pasture. Ain't hardly nobody asking for me no more, so all I got to do is think. Well I been doin' a lot of it lately and I'm all thunk out. Now I want to do some talkin'."

About then is when the waitress showed up with our dinner. My steak was big enough that it was spilling over both sides of the plate. There was barely room for my potato, which could have been a meal by itself.

When Lou said earlier that "she could eat," she wasn't kidding. "Her usual" was a side of ribs and a bucket of beans. She laid into those ribs like she was some kind a roughneck. I watched in awe as she worked through the side and then through that pot. I worked on my steak, which was so raw I thought it was still fighting for its life, and tried to work my way through the potato. It amazed me that before I was half way through my meal, Lou was done with hers and pouring herself another drink.

I pushed my plate back getting ready to continue our conversation. Only Lou was eying my steak. I was more than curious as to what she would do, so I asked her if she wanted to try my steak. She didn't even look up but slid the plate across the table and started in on it. I poured myself a shot, betting she'd be done with my steak before the whisky hit my stomach. I was almost right.

Finally she pushed the plate aside and I poured her another shot. Just as the glass hit the table a fight broke out near the front of the saloon. Presently our waitress appeared and whispered something into Lou's ear.

"You better get out of here Alex," Lou told me. "Peg just told me Reynolds showed up with some of his roughnecks. She knows that if we are seen together there could be trouble."

I didn't wait to find out. Expecting I may have to make a fast exit, I had chosen a table close to the back door. I threw some cash on the table and I asked Lou, "When shall we meet again?" But she was already up and working her way to the bar. Lou was a fixture around here so nobody paid her much mind.

I ducked out the back and made my way up the alley

to Fourth Street. I'd parked my rig there behind the old bank. I made it home without a hitch, but had trouble sleeping that night. My head was spinning with this new information and with the possibilities of where it might lead. I decided I needed to write it all down because who knew if I would live through the next few days.

Too many people were coming up dead and I probably seemed to be asking too many questions. If I didn't make it, I wanted to make sure somebody would have a clue as to what happened. I wrote down all the details then sealed it in an envelope addressed to myself at my ma's place. She was still alive and doing well. She would take the letter and place it in a box in the shed. I had instructed her to do so. I knew that in my business things could happen quickly and that I could end up dead at any time.

Investigative journalism was a new thing. There were dangers in obtaining information others may want kept quiet. I had received threatening letters before. They were delivered to the paper, never signed, always anonymous. I decided to keep a secret journal of all my discoveries. I would just write myself letters and ma would hide them away. Ma was wise in her ways and knew not to ask what was in them and I never told her.

When I got to the paper the next day, my boss, a Scot named Mac told me there had been another killing at the Riggins last night. He said he wanted me to go snoop around and see what I could find out. I wanted to tell him about my experience with Lou but didn't want to put him in danger. No, I would wait this one out and see where the leads took me.

I found myself back at the Riggins that morning before the sun was barely peeking over the horizon. It amazed me that the saloon was as full then as it had been last night. It seemed that as soon as one shift left for work, the next crew would show up to blow off some steam and relax their tired and stiff muscles with a few shots of booze. To my astonishment, Lou was at the bar with a shot in her hand, talking to Reynolds or Three-Finger Jack, whatever his name was. When she recognized me she simple looked the other way as if she didn't even know me. I walked up to the far end of the bar, beckoned for the bartender to come over and asked for a beer. I wanted to just sit and listen to the conversations. The saloon had been a melting pot of information ever since the days of the old west, and if you hung around long enough, you could find out almost anything you wanted to know, and many things you didn't.

Foul Play at the Riggins

My hunch was right and soon some guy started talking about the stabbing that took place the night before. It seemed that the fight broke out about the time that Three-Finger Jack arrived. He had three of his thugs with him. As the story went, apparently one of them had purposely knocked one unsuspecting roughneck into another. This erupted into a bar brawl. When it was over Andrew McCracken lay dead on the floor.

Andrew had owned a plot of land west of town nudged up against Kettleman Hills. McCracken was contracted with one of the smaller oil companies as a wildcatter. Many of these companies were owned and bankrolled by corporations of unknown investors. McCracken had been schooled in geology specializing in geothermal exploration at University of Berkeley and had a good understanding of where the oil was. He was well liked among his team and had a very good success percentage at wildcat wells.

Men like McCracken were in high demand because

wells were going in like hot cakes. There was a lot of money flowing in from investors on the east coast and even as far away as England. All were looking to profit off of the black gold. Whoever employed the sharpest minds in the field of geothermal exploration would prove to develop the most profitable wells.

The word around town was that Old Man Hicks had tried to hire Andrew McCracken as his personal land consultant, and McCracken had turned him down. Coalinga was a relatively young town, wild as they come with thousands of fortune seekers coming and going at any given time. Fortunes were won and lost in the blink of an eye. People would show up dead or disappear without a trace every day. It was more than speculated that the desert sands surrounding the town had become laden with more and more unmarked graves, as the greed of the untrustworthy fortune seekers grew.

I had to believe that the death of McCracken was a planned event. I couldn't prove anything yet, of course, but was suspicious of Three-Finger Jack and his crew. I was figuring Hicks wanted McCracken on his payroll or on no one else's. Hicks, who owned much of the land surrounding the area, had thrown his weight around to get his way and was apparently beginning to believe himself above the law. In fact, he had been operating that way for quite some time.

Also, McCracken's own homestead was well suited for exploration. It was likely he bought wisely eventually planning to spud in his own wells. McCracken was from back east and I suspected he came from money. He had attended the University of Berkeley and then moved to Coalinga, buying a substantial piece of land when he did.

I had interviewed McCracken a few months back. He had reported that by the lay of the land he believed Coalinga possessed one of the largest bodies of crude oil in the United States. He believed, based on the geography of the land, that there were certain land-marks representing the most feasible access to the oil. He was working on a report for the Bureau of Land Management that would spell out the strategic plan for the next 20 to 30 years.

There was plenty of drilling going on though. Many a well was producing large amounts of crude. Many wildcatters acted on impulse wanting to get more rigs in the ground before the other guy. This often proved foolish. McCracken's report was deemed vital infor-mation, and whoever owned that report would control the oil fields. Besides that, drilling a dry well was very costly, not only in man hours, but also in expense and time. No one wanted to waste either.

When my article broke following the interview, the whole town erupted like a bunch of mad hornets whose nest had been kicked. McCracken's expertise, opinions, and services were in high demand. Every land owner or investor wanted his input as to where the most likely spots were to drill. Finally, McCracken and his wife were forced to leave town for a while to let things settle down. It was believed they went back east to visit family. They had just returned two days ago, and now he was dead.

I was sitting at the bar taking it all in when a rough-neck burst through the batwings and announced that the McCracken ranch house had burned to the ground. He said that apparently McCracken's wife had died in the fire. At that, the whole bar burst in to a cacophony of anger and astonishment. Heather McCracken was a well-liked young lady. She had the qualities of a Southern belle to her. She was very beautiful, tall and slender, had long dark hair, deep blue eyes, her skin was as white as milk and when she smiled the whole roomed seemed to become brighter. She had moved out here from South Carolina once Andrew had finished school and settled in. It was thought that she was with child and this only made matters worse.

My immediate suspicion was that whoever killed McCracken was also responsible for the burning down of his house. Whether or not the death of Heather was intentional or not would be a question that needed to be answered. The death of men was commonplace in this town but when someone as lovely and beautiful as Heather McCracken was murdered, a line was crossed. No one was willing to let this go unnoticed. But whether or not the seemingly corrupt powers that be would embrace this position or would overlook it would be something to discover.

Andrew McCracken had an office up on Third Street above the Wells Fargo Building. I decided I would stroll up there and see what I could find. I glanced at Lou on my way out the door, she noticed me and then closed her eyes looking away. What were her thoughts? I definitely needed to speak to her again, and soon.

When I got to McCracken's office, Sheriff Murray was already there. When he heard me walk in to the room, he jumped as if caught in some act. He looked up at me and said, "Hello, McCoy, on it already are ya?" Murray was an Irishman recently elected to office. His family had migrated to New York when he was a small boy, then he relocated to Coalinga when the boom began. I didn't like Murray and he didn't like me. I wasn't sure who his employer really was – the State of California or perhaps Hicks himself.

I noticed the room looked ransacked, his desk was torn apart and his files were all over the floor. "What do you think happened here Sheriff?" I asked, not expecting any version of the truth.

"Looks like some common thief looking for money," he replied.

"Any sign of the land survey report McCracken was working on?" I asked.

Murray stopped for a minute as if caught off guard. "What report would that be?" he asked in a toxic undertone. When he asked that question, he paused, stood erect, looked straight at me, his teeth and eyes displaying no friendliness at all. I knew I would get nowhere with Murray, so I left him to his debauchery. He wasn't a stupid man and would be aware of what McCracken was working on. He would know that the person who possessed those papers would hold the key to the fortunes of the oil fields.

When my article broke in the paper the next morning there was an electric feeling to the town. The only ways for communications like this to travel were by word of mouth or by print. If you didn't frequent Fifth Street, you would miss a lot of the chat about the criminality that was part of the everyday goings on. My weekly column eventually came to be titled, "It Happened on Fifth Street."

The news of the fire and of the death of Heather and her unborn child almost created a riot. Many of the good citizens of Coalinga gathered at the courthouse demanding that Sheriff Murray look into this and find the culprit. Murray appeared on the steps raising his hand to quiet the crowd. He stated that he was looking into the fire, and that so far didn't believe there was any foul play. He said his deputies were out at the McCracken place as he spoke, and that he would inform the crowd of any of his findings as soon as he had finished the investigation.

Angry shouts and allegations came from the crowd, and when someone mentioned Hicks' name, there was an uproar. Murray raised his hands to quiet the crowd, finally turning away he disappeared into the court-house.

I realized I had been negligent in my duties and de-cided I better get out to the McCracken place and nose around. I jumped into my model T and started up the road that lead up the Peachtree Grade toward McCracken's house.

I arrived at the McCracken place about noon. The Deputies were two men, both of Irish descent and both of suspect background. As I pulled up, Flannery, a red-haired, ill-tempered stump of a man blocked my approach, snarling, "There's an investigation going on here McCoy. Go back the way you come!"

"The good people of Coalinga are very upset about this Flannery. I believe it best to let me look around. You wouldn't want me to write about how uncoopera-tive the law was, would you? The people in town are wanting answers and I believe they trust me more than the law right now."

There had been much talk about an association be-tween Hicks and Murray. There were rumors that they had known each other prior to coming to Coalinga. I didn't mention this, wanting to keep an ace in the hole.

"You better watch where you are sticking your nose McCoy, or it might get broken," Flannery threatened more than stated.

Just then Deputy O'Malley appeared from behind the barn with a shovel in his hand. "All done here, Flann...." He stopped short when he saw me, looking kind of guilty. "What's he doing here?" O'Malley demanded from Flannery.

"Sticking his nose where it shouldn't be," Flannery told him. "Now if you know what's good for you McCoy, you'll go back to where you come from. It might be good for your health to start reporting on the upcoming quilting bee."

I thought it best for my health to head back to town so I just turned, jumped into my rig and headed for home. As I looked in my rearview mirror I could see Flannery and O'Malley in what appeared to be a heated conversation. I was very curious as to what their report of the fire would reveal, if anything.

One thing for sure though, I planned on finding out what O'Malley was using that shovel for.

When I got back to the paper, Mac met me and asked me to come into his office. I followed him in and sat down in the rickety wooden chair across from his desk. "Just got a call from a friend in South Carolina, runs The Herald in Charleston. Apparently McCracken's dad is a bigwig out there. Owns a few plantations, survived the war okay. In fact, according to my contact, came out on top. He's not happy about the death of his son, nor his daughter in law. The fact that Heather was pregnant was unknown to him, and when he was told, let me just say, he's not taking it lying down. McCracken's body is being shipped back east along with any remains of Heather. The old man is sending his attorney out here to settle his affairs. The old man asked for you specifically, said his son mentioned you a couple of times and told him you could be trusted and that you are fair man. Got to tell you, Alex, be careful. I think this whole town is about to blow up. You might consider sending Beth and your kids out of town for a few weeks. There is big money involved here and they won't be stopped easily."

I thanked Mac for the heads up and told him I'd speak to Beth about it. Her family was from a small town in the valley called Woodville. Her family farmed cotton there. They'd been there since about 1853. They usually summered in the mountains at a lake called Huntington. I thought this would be a good enough excuse for the family to go camping at the lake.

Beth's family had arrived in America around 1634. They pioneered what is now Connecticut, fighting the famous Pequot Indians for their land. Her grandfather, Julius Orton, joined the cavalry to fight in the Mexican-American War around 1847, and he landed in Nevada about the time gold was discovered at Sutter's Mill. He ended up prospecting up in and around Hang Town, now called Placerville. They called it Hang Town because there was at least one public hanging a day, but usually more. Seemed there were more thieves than there were prospectors around town, but between them all, the life expectancy of the good people of Hang Town was short. Julius Orton was one of the fortunate ones, for not only did he actually managed to strike it rich, but he lived long enough to then move to a small coastal town in California called Santa Cruz, having purchased 20,000 acres there.

His fortune was short-lived though, for as fate would have it, he was swindled out of the whole lot when California became a state. The story goes that some shady underhanded bureaucrat was able to file a claim to the land before Julius did, and the man's friends in Mariposa, the state capital at the time, ruled in his favor. It seemed an amazing story to me, that a man could have lived through the Mexican-American War, struck it rich in the wild and woolly gold fields of California, lived to talk about it, and then settle down to raise a family only to have it all stolen out from under him by some bureaucrat. I was beginning to see a resemblance between the gold strike of the 1850s and the oil strikes here in Coalinga. It seemed that wherever there was money or the prospect of riches, the evils of man would surface to steal them. I marveled again at how some men would work so hard to underhandedly acquire the hard-earned wealth of another, when if they had just focused their own efforts on a legitimate cause they could create their own wealth.

Regardless, since Julius Orton had fought in the war, the government allotted him 160 acres, or a quarter of a section of land. After the loss of his land in Santa Cruz, he took his wife, Elizabeth Bixby, and moved to the Woodville area and took up farming. At any rate Beth had a large family there and would be well protected.

I was up early the next morning and on my way up to McCracken's place. I thought I'd look around while the dirt would still be fresh. About five miles up the Peachtree Grade was a little road that led to his place. The road took off to the left and bordered the foothills and the desert. His house was built at the beginning of a box canyon and had some of the only shade trees around standing guard. He had built a modest ranch house under the trees, which provided the much-needed shade. There had been an old sheepherder's shack on the land which was now gone, but the old barn was in pretty good shape. I parked my rig under the trees and started investigating the barn. It was clear that the barn had been gone through pretty well recently, and I'm pretty sure it was the work of O'Malley and Flannery.

I started nosing around behind the barn and sure enough found fresh dirt indicating something was recently buried. Finding the shovel O'Malley had left, I started in on the spot. Within about ten minutes, I uncovered the body of the McCracken's old dog. I was wondering what would make O'Malley a caring enough fellow to give the poor old dog a decent burial, when I located the bullet hole on his side where his heart would be. Now I understood where O'Malley's kindness, or lack of, was coming from. Deciding I'd keep my discovery to myself for now, I reburied the dog and made my way back to town.

That afternoon I was at my desk making some notes when a man named Bloomberg knocked on my door. "Hello, Frank," I said, "to what do I owe this visit too?"

"Nothin' really," Bloomberg said. "I was going to head up the grade and try some fishing below the spring tomorrow, thought you might want to go with me." Bloomberg was a businessman in town and of questionable loyalty. Fact is, he followed the buck, shifting alliances as the wind blew. I believed he had alliances with Hicks himself but he was often known to associate with Mayor Adams. Adams had arrived in town several years ago and seemed to have his pot on many fires. I was very curious as to where this might lead so I agreed to go. I told Bloomberg I'd pick him up at 5:00 the next morning. I liked fishing anyway and was curious how the spring was producing. There wasn't much water in the foothills but Miller's Spring produced well, and there were usually some good size trout to be caught if one knew how.

I picked Frank up at 5:00 the next morning and we headed out of town. Frank talked about nothing particular and seemed a bit nervous. I just let him fidget, enjoying the show.

We'd been on the road about 30 minutes and the sun was beginning to peak over the eastern horizon when Frank turned the conversation to some of the recent events in town. He talked about the death of Andrew and Heather McCracken and what a shame it was. He also commented on the increased killings around Whisky Row and what a sad day it was when people's lives got in the way of progress. I asked him what kind of progress he was speaking of, and said it seemed like the progress he was talking about was taking on the form of thievery, dishonesty, and murder.

With that he became very quiet. He looked at me for a minute then began, "McCoy you know I have always liked you."

I knew this was a lie but decided to let it play out.

"You have a way of sticking your nose where it shouldn't be. You know me, Alex, I'm a businessman and well connected with the powers that be in town. I work for myself and am aligned with no single entity. I prefer to keep my options open."

"That's what I like about you, Frank," I said, "as honest as the day is long and always looking out for your friends."

Frank paused for a minute then said in a rather flat but poignant tone, "McCoy, you're a smart man. There are things at stake in this town that are bigger than both you and me. You are well liked here. You've helped make this town what it is. I respect what you stand for.

The only thing I am worried about McCoy, is that you don't know when to quit. You keep stickin' your nose where it don't belong."

Bloomberg paused for a minute, pulled out a cigar, and went through the process off biting off the end, moistening its leaves by rolling it on his tongue, then lighting a match, sucking the flame into the end until it began to glow. He seemed to enjoy himself, thinking he was a big man around town.

After filling the rig with enough smoke to choke a goat he said to me in a seemingly sincere yet somehow sarcastic and threatening tone, "Ran into Beth and the kids the other day at the market. Boy, those youngins are growing fast."

Pausing again, he drew on his stogie, then as he held the cigar in front of his face and seemed to be inspecting the roll of the leaves he mentioned, "I think you might want to consider what's best for the health of your family, McCoy. It seems newspaper work could be detrimental to their well-being." With that he was quiet, and I got his message loud and clear. I didn't respond, but was thinking fast.

I owned a .38 Colt that I had purchased on a fishing expedition up in Alaska back in '06. I had just turned 21, and seeking adventure, had hired on as a crew on a salmon boat heading up to Ketchikan. That was quite an adventure, but those stories are best kept for another day. Anyway, the Colt was the same model that Teddy

Roosevelt carried up San Juan Hill with his Rough Riders, his famous run during the Spanish American War. I always kept it hanging from my steering column more for novelty than for protection.

Suddenly a jackrabbit jumped up to our left and started running not ten feet from my rig. As I was still thinking, taking in what Bloomberg was implying, by impulse pulled out that .38 and fired a shot at that rabbit. By pure luck that bullet hit that rabbit in its rear hunches and dropped it in its tracks. It happened very fast. I couldn't even tell you that it was a conscious act on my part. Regardless, I didn't say a thing or look at Frank. I just put that gun away and continued driving on up to the fishing spot.

Frank remained very quiet for what seemed like several minutes, when he did speak it was to ask me to pull the car over for a minute. I obliged and as I pulled to a stop, he opened the door and hurried out of the car, commenting that he seemed to have developed car sickness. He barely made it out of the car when he gave up his breakfast. He wretched several times, emptying anything and everything that his stomach had to disgorge. After a minute I exited the car and walked over to where his spent body slumped against the side of the hill.

He held himself up against a boulder and as I looked at him he appeared very pale and I could see the formation of beads of perspiration escaping his body. This was odd, because it was not yet 6:00 and the hot desert sun was just peaking over the Sierra to the east, not yet baking the earth.

"What seems to be the matter, Frank?" I asked in the best sympathetic tone I could muster.

"That windy stretch of road got the best of me, or maybe it was something I had to eat," he replied. Then after a minute of trying to compose himself, he added that he'd forgot about an important appointment he had that afternoon in town and thought it best that we postpone the fishing for another day. I was agreeable and so we headed back to town. Frank just sat there, a quiet and polite passenger. What I found interesting was that in the weeks that followed, the stream of threatening letters to me and to my family seemed to magically dry up.

Being a cautious man, I decided that a short trip to the mountains would be a good idea. We packed up the car and the family and headed for Huntington Lake. It was a beautiful spot at about 7,000 feet on the west side of the Sierra. Beth's family was surprised to see us. We enjoyed a nice cool couple of days by the lake, swimming, fishing, playing cribbage, and throwing horseshoes.

The Ortons were a large clan, and Beth's Uncles Virgil, Bert, and Norman were always arguing and trying to best each other in anything and everything they did. They were always creating games or contests which involved things like swimming across the lake, or racing around it, splitting wood, throwing hatchets, canoe racing or some other crazy challenge. At night we'd sit around the fire while Virgil and Norman would entertain us with Vaudeville style comedy of limericks and music. It was quite enjoyable and a nice break from the tension and drama of the Coalinga oil fields. After a few days of rest and relaxation, I packed up to return home and told Beth and the kids I would pick them up in a week or so after they arrived back at her folks' place in Woodville.

George McMann, Esquire

Upon my arrival back in Coalinga, it seemed like all hell had broken loose. When I asked Mac about it, he told me that a couple days after I left, a big fancy Packard pulled into town and stopped in front of the International Hotel, which was located across the street from *The Record*. Mac said that he observed the chauffeur, who had the body of a prize fighter and a face to prove it, open the rear door, allowing a very well dressed little man to step out onto the street. He described the man to have stood just over five feet, and was wearing a black pinstriped three-piece suit, spats, a derby hat, and had a well-trained, well-trimmed, black mustache which culminated in a sharp point on each side of his nose.

The man stepped up on the sidewalk and sauntered into the hotel as if he owned the place. It seemed that the town stood still for a minute because all eyes followed this would-be gentleman and his goon.

Mac said that curiosity had got the best of him so he wandered over to the hotel and asked Schmitty, the hotel proprietor, who the stiff was. Mac had a good reputation with the reputable people in town and Schmitty was one of them. There was a faction of folks in town who wanted to raise a family here and didn't tolerate the goings-on that occurred around Fifth Street.

Anyway, Schmitty turned the hotel ledger around and turned away as if to check the mail. This allowed Mac the time necessary to peer at the last signature. It was written in a beautifully elegant scroll, and it clearly read "George M. McMann, Esquire." His goon had not signed in and by the looks of the man Mac questioned whether he could have if he'd wanted to.

Mac went back to *The Record* and decided to call his friend at the *Charleston Herald* and see what he could dig up. As he had suspected, McMann was none other than the fastidious attorney to old man Angus McCracken. Mac's contact told him that even though he was a wimpy looking fellow, he had the temper of the devil and the bite of a scorpion. He said that he was very dangerous and very smart he also warned that nothing got by him. He mentioned that he believed *The Record* would be his first stop because Andrew had told his father about Alexander McCoy and that he was a man to be trusted. He also added that the big guy, McMann's chauffeur, was called Rex, no last name was known, only that his name was a homonymic indication of what he left in his path. Mac got the point and so did I.

Just as Mac finished filling me in on the details the jingle of the bells hanging above the front door of *The Record* sounded. Mac got up from his desk putting his hand up to caution me to wait.

"Good morning, Mr. McMann, what can I do for you?" Mac started.

"Good morning, Mr. McDougall. It is my understanding that Mr. McCoy is back in town. I would like to schedule an appointment to speak to him at his earliest convenience."

I couldn't stand the suspense and against my better judgment stepped through the doorway announcing myself. "I'm Alexander McCoy. Whom do I have the pleasure of meeting?"

Mac turned to look at me with a furrowed brow, no doubt disapproving of my action.

"Mr. McCoy, my name is George M. McMann, esquire to the McCracken Organization. I am here to settle Andrew's estate and to handle any and all loose ends regarding his death, as well as his personal and business associations. The sheriff suggested that Andrew's death was circumstantial to one of the frequent brawls which take place in the Riggins as well as many of the other establishments of ill repute found along your unsavory Fifth Street. To my understanding, Andrew did not drink nor had ever set foot in a saloon in his entire life. Andrew was a God-fearing man. He loved his wife, Heather, very much and would never do anything to jeopardize his family. If you don't mind Mr. McCoy I would like to speak to you in private. Is there a place we might meet?"

My first inclination was to tell Mr. McMann that Mac was trustworthy and could be helpful, but then decided I wanted to protect him with immunity. I mentioned I could meet him tomorrow around twelve o'clock.

"Excuse me for not making myself clear Mr. McCoy, I would like to have our meeting now."

When I told him I had appointments this afternoon, his response was direct. "I see, Mr. McCoy. Why don't you ask Mr. McDougall to assist you with your appointments?"

"Mr. McDougall is not my assistant Mr. McMann, he is my boss," I replied.

"I'm sure he wouldn't mind assisting you under the circumstances." Turning his attention to Mac he continued, "Would you Mr. McDougall?" McMann said directing more than asking.

Mac kind of stumbled an answer which seemed to say, "Of course."

"Great, that is settled. Where can we speak in private?" McMann asked.

"Please, use my office," Mac offered. "I have work to do anyway."

"How very kind of you Mr. McDougall. Your cooperation will not go unnoticed."

Mac left us and we moved into his office to settle in, but I soon found my path to Mac's desk was blocked by the goon. It amazed me that throughout this whole ordeal, the big guy had gone virtually unnoticed. McMann's presence was so big and his intention so powerful that nothing seemed to get in his way.

McMann proceeded to seat himself at Mac's desk, then gestured that I sit in the old rickety wooden chair I had been so accustomed to. I swore to myself that someday I was going to buy myself a comfortable chair for that office. I relished in the thought of burning the thing as firewood.

"Mr. McCoy, I assume you are aware of why I am here. There is no doubt in my mind but that Andrew's death was intentional. You had published an article about the interview you had with Andrew, and about his knowledge regarding the lay of the oil fields. Understand me Mr. McCoy, the Old Man does not hold you in contempt, and in fact appreciated the kindness you had shown to his son and his wife, Heather. He was very proud of Andrew and of his accomplishments.

"He believes as I do that foul play has entered into Coalinga's oil business and his intention is that I get to the bottom of it and handle any and all aspects of the depravity.

"First, let me tell you that I have been to the Land Surveyor's Office and have secured proper title to Andrew's property near Kettleman Hills. It seems that an alias corporation had already put in a quick claim to the property contesting the original title. I have men tracking down this would be corporation, and should have some answers by the end of the week.

"What I need from you, Mr. McCoy, is your full cooperation and confidence. You see, Mr. McCoy, I am not a patient man and in fact have quite a full plate back home. Being here in this God-forsaken desert is not pleasing to me. The heat causes me to break out in hives, which makes my patience even shorter. The sooner I get out of California, the better for all concerned; well, except for any man I find contrary to the interests of Andrew's well-being or the security of the McCracken holdings."

I was amazed at the way this man spoke, he seemed to just wave his hand and anything he wished was at his command. I couldn't help feeling a bit sorry for anyone who would be found to have crossed the McCracken family. I was thinking about how crowded the nearby desert may become with shallow graves by the time McMann and his goon, Rex, departed.

As I studied the situation, I was drawn to the man sitting in front of me. He was a petite little man with chiseled features. His nose was thin and came to a sharp point. He had deep blue eyes set deep in his face, accented by well groomed, black eyebrows. His mustache was well waxed and was exactly 90 degrees to the horizon. His lips were pencil thin and turned slightly up at the sides. He had high cheekbones and a distinct scar about two inches long running from just below his left lower lip disappearing under his chin. Looking at his hands I noticed that they reminded me of those of an elegant southern lady. They were well manicured, appeared to be soft as a lamb's skin and as pale as a Southern belle's. I briefly thought perhaps he developed into the wrong sex at birth. Thinking twice though, he had a mind that was as ruthless, cunning, and deadly as a rattlesnake, which complemented this rather complex individual.

He interrupted my reverie. "Mr. McCoy, would you please answer my question?" This was accompanied by a guttural noise as well as a change of position from the goon.

"I'm sorry, Mr. McMann, could you please repeat your question?" I was beginning to regret not heeding Mac's warning about staying out of sight in the first place.

"I'll ask you again, Mr. McCoy, to tell me everything you know about the death of my client. Anything you believe will help me finish my business here so I can return to Charleston."

"Well, Mr. McMann, I'm not sure where to begin. This town is exploding with men coming and going at any time. Whether Andrew's death was an accident, or perpetrated as you may suggest, is the business of the sheriff and not of *The Record*." I felt proud of myself for such a well thought out reply. Well for a minute anyway.

McMann reached over and picked up a picture of Mac's family sitting on his desk and studied it for what seemed like an eternity. Without making a comment about them he took out a handkerchief, wiped off his fingerprints and any others there may have been and placed it back in the exact spot it had been sitting on.

He looked at me with those sharp, deep blue eyes and calmly stated, "Tell me about the lady who is known as Lou."

"I'm sorry?" I replied as a question, hinting that I wasn't sure what he was referring to.

"Please don't underestimate me, Mr. McCoy, or Mr. Angus McCracken's intentions. Do you think he would leave his only son to forage in the wilderness of the California foothills all alone? You see, Mr. McCoy, I have had eyes on the ground here for some time. It is quite unfortunate for their owners that they ultimately failed in their duty of protecting young Andrew and his family. I was at least able to extract every bit of information I needed from them before they left the employment of the McCracken organization."

I couldn't help but wonder how this statement affected the increase in the number of inhabitants of our shallow desert cemetery.

McMann continued, "It is my suspicion that Andrew was either lured to, or escorted to the Riggins that night against his will. I believe the murder was premeditated and the Riggins was used to cover up the intentions of the assailants. This is further evidenced by the fact that my men were detained that evening. I am told that a deputy by the name of O'Malley stopped the two as they were making their way to locate young Andrew. Apparently they were missing a taillight on their vehicle. The driver assured me that the light was working at the time. It seems someone had fingered the two. Careless of them I must say.

"One of the boys said they saw a lady of the night, a rather old one, approach you on the street the day before Andrew was killed. You see, Mr. McCoy, we were looking out for you as well."

I felt a chill going down my spine, I had not suspected this at all.

"So tell me, what of this Lou? What should you be telling me?"

"I've known Lou for a long time, Mr. McMann. She keeps me informed on the goings on around Fifth Street. As I'm sure you know, I have an article named just that, 'It Happened on Fifth Street'. It makes for a good story, and while the good people of Coalinga may not venture down to Fifth Street, they do like a good story about the wild and woolly west."

"As do we all, Mr. McCoy, as do we all," McMann agreed, then added, "I'm not looking for a story, Mr. McCoy, I'm looking for information." He pulled out a gold watch which resided in his right-hand vest pocket, a gold chain connected it to the left. Pressing the top of the stem it snapped open for him to gaze at. His mustache twitched as he returned the watch to his pocket, at which point he abruptly stood up and said, "Stay close, Mr. McCoy, I will have more questions for you soon. He started toward the door then paused looking at me, "And please, Mr. McCoy, don't waste my time." Rex glided to the door escorting Mr. McMann out. Rex hesitated before he followed merely gazing into my eyes. He didn't have to say a word; his point was well taken.

I marveled at the two, so different in stature. Rex, as big as an ox, moved as smoothly as a ballerina, his feet hardly making a sound as he glided across the floor. McMann, who fit the description of a dandy yet had the personality of a python.

Mac appeared at the door and walked over to sit in his seat. I looked at him and announced, "I believe Coalinga is about to get on the map. That is one dangerous man, and whoever gets in his way won't be there for long. He means business."

I felt I had to tell Mac a bit of what I knew. It was too much for me to think about alone and Mac was a very wise and experienced mind. I told him that there were things I should keep to myself for the time being. I did tell him that if anything did happen to me to please contact my mother. I told him she would be of help. I left it at that not wanting to say too much.

The Midnight Call

I got a call about midnight that night. It was an anony-mous call which simply said I was to drive to the inter-section of the highway 198 (the Peachtree Grade) and Franklin Road. Franklin Road was located in the oil fields, about as remote as it could get.

I jumped into my rig and started up the road. There was no moon so it was pitch dark. When I approached the turn off to Franklin I became aware of a distant glow. If I didn't know better I would have said it was a fire.

As I eased over the small rise in the desert I saw I was right. I pulled up to the tail end of a car fire. Sheriff Murray had just arrived and was getting out of his car as I pulled up.

He shined a light in my eye then snapped the question, "What the hell are you doing here, McCoy?"

"Got an anonymous tip, Sheriff. What do we got?"

Together we approached the vehicle. Murray stopped short and soon I understood why. This was O'Malley's patrol car. We could see the driver's window was shattered, like it had been shot through. On closer inspection I noticed what looked like two bullet holes in the driver's door. There was blood on the seat, and it was clear that someone had died there. From what I knew after talking to McMann, I believed this was delivering a message.

"Keep this under you hat for a while, McCoy. I need to do some snooping around and some thinking," Murray told me.

"Okay, Sheriff, I can sit on this until Wednesday's edition but no longer."

"Good enough," Murray said. "Someone's going to pay for this."

"Perhaps someone just did," I remarked.

Murray stopped dead in his tracks, looked at me and said, "What are you talking about McCoy? What do you know?"

"It just seemed odd to me that O'Malley happened to be out at McCracken's place when I got out there after the fire. I couldn't understand why he was carrying a shovel, so I went back out and did some nosing around. I just couldn't understand how McCracken's dog ended up in a shallow grave with a bullet piercing his heart."

With that I turned and got back into my car and headed straight to the International. I parked around the back so I wouldn't draw attention.

Let Dead Dogs Lie

Before heading up to McMann's room, I located the Packard and felt the engine cover; as I suspected, it was warm. When I knocked on McMann's door, Rex opened it almost immediately.

"Good evening, Mr. McCoy," McMann said. "I've been expecting you, I see you got my message."

"Your message?" I replied innocently.

"Why yes," he replied. "I had asked Rex to go over to your house and see if we could meet. He mentioned you were not there so he left a note. Where on earth would you be going so late at night, Mr. McCoy? You were not visiting one of the inhabitants of Fifth Street, were you? I know your wife is at the lake, but still, Mr. McCoy, show a little restraint."

How he knew the whereabouts of my family hit hard in the pit of my stomach. But one thing I was certain of was that I was on the right side of the equation.

This man was a master, assuming that Rex was responsible for what happened to O'Malley, which I did, his alibi was iron clad. I had no doubt there would be a note awaiting me on my door when I got home. It would be an invitation from Mr. McMann to join him for a nightcap. That would explain the warm engine and explain why Rex had left the hotel. Clever.

"A shame about Officer O'Malley," I remarked. "He was almost honest."

"I'm afraid I haven't met the man," McMann stated. "What can you tell me about him?"

I didn't bother telling about the fire; I wasn't that much of a greenhorn. He knew I didn't miss much.

"Mr. McMann," I started, "I was one of the first people out at Andrew's place following the fire. When I arrived, I came upon Deputies Flannery and O'Malley investigating the area. What struck me was O'Malley appearing from behind the barn with a shovel in his hand. He looked shocked to see me and demanded to know what I was doing there. When I mentioned that I was investigating the fire, he told me this was a police investigation and that I should leave immediately."

I told McMann that I did leave, but that I returned later to figure out what the shovel was used for. I told him about the grave, the dog, and the bullet wound. I was surprised to see a brief moment of grief flash across McMann's face.

"That would have been Rudy, the family dog," he explained, a note of sadness in his voice. "He grew up in

South Carolina. Andrew brought him out with him after he graduated Berkeley." McMann composed himself, taking a sip of his tea.

"I ran into Sheriff Murray out on Franklin Road and had to tell him about the encounter with O'Malley at the McCracken house. I believe Murray will be heading out that way and thought you might want to be around when he showed up."

McMann stood up and thanked me for my information. Rex opened the door, escorting me out. As I headed home, I saw the Packard making its way up toward Peachtree Grade. When I arrived home, there was a note on my door on George M. McMann's letterhead requesting I visit him ASAP at his hotel room at the International.

It has been said that curiosity killed the cat, and well, I guess I was about to find out if I could avoid that fate. No later than the second my rump hit the pillow on my easy chair did I jump up. Gathering my coat and hat, I was out the door. I jumped into my rig and started up the back road that would lead me to the southern end of the McCracken property. I was pretty sure Sheriff Murray would be on his way, and I couldn't resist watching what came down.

It was more of a trail than a road, but I had traveled it many times because there was a small spring that flowed out of a small box canyon, probably the only decent water in the area, and I'd stopped there a number of times for a drink. As I drove along the side of the hill, I could see the headlights of an approaching car. I cut my lights and made the rest of the way on foot.

I reached a small rise behind the barn just as the sheriff was pulling up. I could see the Packard to the left of the barn parked beside one of the few trees on the property. There was the occasional glow of what I guessed was Rex's cigarette as he stood behind the car.

Shortly, Murray pulled up, opened the car door and went around to his trunk. He pulled out a shovel and a light then started searching for the fresh mound of dirt that I had described. After a few minutes of searching in the dark he came across the mound. Setting the light down he started digging.

After a few minutes of digging he seemed to have hit the carcass in the shallow grave. Rex choose that time to make his presence known.

"This is private property, mister, and I'm looking down the barrel of an 1873 Winchester repeating rifle. I should add that I rarely miss."

Sheriff Murray stood perfectly still before announcing himself.

"I am Sheriff Patrick Murray, I am in the process of investigating a murder. I'd advise you to lower your rifle and come out in the open where I can see you."

"It's okay, Rex," McMann said from the side of the barn. "I know the sheriff. I believe he is here to assist in the investigation of Andrew and Heather's murders."

"Who said anything about the McCrackens?" Murray retorted angrily. "I'm talking about my deputy!"

I think Murray saw his mistake as the words left his mouth.

"Sheriff Murray," McMann began as both he and Rex approached him from different angles. "I don't quite understand how the digging of a hole on my client's property and the death of your deputy, Mr. O'Malley, have a connection. Will you please enlighten me as to what they have in common?"

Murray was silent for a moment, then stated rather weakly, "This is police business, McMann. I advise you stay out of it."

"Mr. Murray, I must say, here you are trespassing in the middle of the night digging for oil or some other thing without a search warrant, and without address-ing me prior to the event. I believe the documents I had delivered to you on my arrival clearly stated that I am the custodian of Andrew McCracken's estate and that any and all actions regarding the property must receive my approval prior to any action. Do you not recall that document I had served on you, Mr. Murray?"

Murray started backing up and stated, "You're right, McMann, I guess I got ahead of myself. I'll be heading back to town and serve notice in the morning." As he turned to leave, he ran right into the bulk of Rex's body. Rex having moved like a panther, undetected by even me.

"I'm interested to see what you were looking for here, Mr. Murray. Why don't you go ahead and finish what you started?"

Murray started to say something when the distinct sound of a '73 Winchester lever being cocked disturbed the night.

"This is not a request, Mr. Murray," McMann declared. "Start digging." The words came as an order, and one to be obeyed.

After about five minutes, Murray had "discovered" the carcass of the old family dog. McMann bent down and poked around a minute then announced the discovery of the bullet hole I had found earlier. McMann looked up at Murray, took a clean silk handkerchief out of his pocket and wiped his hands.

Murray stood there like a kid caught with his hands in the candy jar.

"What do a dead deputy and a dead dog have in common, Mr. Murray? I can't wait to hear what you have to say about this," McMann said. Then he asked Rex to rebury Rudy. The poor dog had three burials so far, more than anyone deserved.

"I found a note on O'Malley's desk at the station. It described this spot. He suspected foul play and was going to investigate in the morning. When I found O'Malley had been killed, I had gone back to his desk to see if there were any leads I could follow up on. I didn't think it worth waking you in the middle of the night, Mr. McMann, and intended on filling you in in the morning."

Not acknowledging Murray's comment regarding the death of O'Malley, McMann commented, "I believe you are correct in suspecting 'foul play' as you call it, Mr. Murray. Although, I suspect we may each have our own description of 'the circumstances'. I suggest you go home now. I'm sure your wife is no doubt wondering about your whereabouts, again." The jab did not get past Murray, but he held his tongue. Murray had a reputation of spending more than one night in a small candle-lit room on the second floor of a shanty on Fifth Street.

After Murray's patrol car disappeared in the distance, McMann said in a rather matter-of-fact tone, "You can come out now, Mr. McCoy. The coast is clear." That he knew I was there didn't surprise me a bit. This man didn't miss a beat and I was beginning to feel very happy about the fact that I was on his good side.

As I stepped out of the shadows brushing the soil off of my clothes, McMann said, "You were right in coming to me, Mr. McCoy. I knew the sheriff was dirty the moment I laid eyes on him. In fact, I had a little investigating done on him and his henchmen while on my train ride out west. Murray was involved in a large embezzlement attempt on a subsidiary of the Rockefeller's organization back east.

The fact that he failed is probably the only reason he is alive today. The fact remains that he and his two deputies are wanted men. There are a couple guys that would grind them up into mincemeat if they were found. Their lives are too important to me just now though. I need to use them to get to the bottom of this whole affair. Tomorrow, I would like to continue our conversation regarding the lady known as Lou. And, Mr. McCoy, please don't make me go to her." He paused indicating to Rex that it was time to go. "Lunch at the International tomorrow, twelve o'clock sharp." With that he turned and walked to his car.

I chose to stay a while, doing some thinking in the conducive night air. I wondered where this would all end. I had decided to take this whole thing on myself, and then McCracken was killed and all hell broke loose. I gave out a sigh, and then decided it was time to turn in. It had been quite an interesting few weeks.

The Informant

The next morning on my way into town, I began to think back on the last few weeks. Things had happened so fast since my first meeting with Lou that I had not really had any time to consider the overall situation.

I was quite sure that McMann would be on Hicks' trail soon, and I believed he would be conducting an investigation on the connections between Three-Finger Jack, Lou, and Hicks. The fact that Hicks was probably the man ultimately responsible for my father's death had not eluded me. The shooting had happened many years ago and my father had been dead some thirteen years, but I owed it to both him and Ma to bring the issue to justice. Just exactly what that would look like I just wasn't yet sure.

On my way to meet McMann at the International, I decided it was time to tell him about the night Andrew was killed and of my affiliation with Lou. I figured he probably already knew most of it anyway or would find out soon enough, but since we were both basically on the same side, we could help each other.

McMann was waiting when I arrived and looked at his watch as I reached the table. Being aware of his penchant for precession I decided to be on time, and I was.

We ordered lunch and then McMann started the ball rolling. "Tell me about Hicks," he said.

I took a sip of coffee deciding where to begin. I stopped wasting time and started from the beginning. I told him about my Pa and the train station, about the robbery or hold up for my pa's horse and buggy. I mentioned that Pa, even though shot in the lung, lived to be fifty years old. When I mentioned that the buggy was found on the grade and that there were signs of oil on it he became particularly interested.

Finally I told him about my meeting with Lou, about her information on Hicks and his possible connection to Pa's death. I mentioned that Hicks had gone to visit Lou that night and that she had cleaned him up. I told him that Hicks told her she was to not speak of that night and that she never had...until that night at the Riggins, the night Andrew McCracken was murdered.

He asked more about Hicks and then about Darwin and Reynolds, and about the nickname, Three-Finger Jack. He seemed fascinated by the story of Joaquin Murrieta and the original Three-Finger Jack and their antics. Apparently McMann was a fan of the old west and other than the dirt and heat, thought he would enjoy exploring a bit. I wasn't sure if this, what I saw as warming up to me, was authentic or just a way to get me to trust him more. I was not going to throw caution to the wind.

I went through the steps leading up to the barroom brawl which left young Andrew dead. I told him that I had liked Andrew and had known him to be an honest and humble man. I had never known him to drink and never seen him anywhere near Fifth Street. I agreed with McMann's theory that he had either been dragged or by gun point brought there against his will. I supposed there could have been something, some kind of information, which could have drawn him there. There were always fights breaking out at the Riggins, as well as every other bar on Fifth Street; it was a way of life, and death. That it would be a perfect backdrop for murder there was no question. Lou told me that a waitress had told her that Reynolds had entered the saloon just minutes before the fight broke out, and in the end one man lay dead. That man was Andrew McCracken.

McMann turned the conversation to Lou and he wanted to know more about her. I told him all I knew which really wasn't much. He suggested I make arrangements for him to meet her, that it would be important for everyone involved that he get some answers. I mentioned I wasn't sure if she would be agreeable.

McMann put his immaculate hand on the table close to mine and looked me straight in the eye and said, "I am a very powerful man, Mr. McCoy. My connections go very deep, to the founders of this country. I have connections and associations even Angus McCracken doesn't know about. I can be a friend to Miss Lou, or I can be a bitter enemy. Go talk to her. Tell her she will come out of this very well if she cooperates. She could end up with the means to retire and settle down in a home in a place of her own choosing.

"Angus McCracken may be many things, but he is a fair man and a southern gentleman. He believes women should be taken care of. He knows of Lou and has given me the power to help he. There is a little cabin next to the old coaling station, I'm sure you know the spot. It is rarely used. Tell her to meet me there at 5:00 am tomorrow; you should come as well. Rex will make sure no one follows either of you."

I spotted Rex across the room. He was watching a shifty looking roughneck who seemed a bit out of place in the International. The man was pretending to be looking at a menu, but I could tell he was trying very hard to hear our conversation. Somehow I felt confident his mouth would not be successful in repeating anything he may have heard.

Rex was an interesting study. I had never seen him eat and had rarely heard him say a word. That he was intelligent was no question. He seemed to have a way of intercepting anything and everything that had to do with the McCrackens' interest. How it came into my mind, I don't know, but the thought was that I would see if I could get Rex to speak before the week was out.

I decided it would be best to send a messenger to contact Lou for me. Murray would be looking for anything
happening around me and McMann, and I assumed
Reynolds would be on the lookout as well. When I
asked Mac and a few others about Reynolds, nobody
seemed to have seen him since Andrew's death. Reynolds had a way of disappearing now and then and
could easily be out of town on business.

I sent a young paperboy named Jimmy down to Fifth
Street selling papers. The headline was the death of
Deputy O'Malley. Apparently, while chasing a suspected thief, he lost control of his patrol car which hit
an oil derrick. The crash caused the car to catch fire and
he was killed in the fire. Sheriff Murray had commented for publication that "O'Malley was a good cop
and that his presence in Coalinga law enforcement
would be sorely missed." I was willing to hold back the
evidence I had seen at the Sheriff's request to assist in
the ongoing investigation.

At any rate the paper sold well and most people bought
it...the story that is. As usual, Lou came out to buy her
copy and as she did, the kid slipped her a note from
me. She winked and tipped him two bits.

This is what the note said: "Dear Lou, I have been in
communication with a man I think you should meet.
He has mentioned that your future was looking brighter. I trust this man. Meet him at the old shack by the
coaling station at 5:00 am tomorrow. You won't be
followed. I'll be there."

The note was on plain paper and unsigned. There was no need, she would know it was from me.

Dry-Hole Charlie Hits the Big One

I thought I would wander over to the Riggins and get some news. There was a lot of excitement going on there. Dutch Henry's company had just landed a big one. His driller was Dry-Hole Charlie, so named for his reputation for picking the wrong place to dig. He had upwards of 1,000 failed wells when he finally hit the big one while employed with Dutch Henry. They had been drilling for a month when they finally hit the payoff. The gusher shot straight up out of the ground in a strong stream, it would probably take them three to four weeks to cap it. This well would likely produce for decades so there was much celebrating to do.

I knew Dutch pretty well; he was a hothead but was a good man. When he saw me come through the doors he immediately beckoned me over and poured me a drink. When big ones came in, it was "drinks for the house" from the one who hit it. Dutch was a good drinker and would not get home until someone carried him, which was usually sometime after noon the next day.

Dutch had a modest company. He was bankrolled by someone back east whose name remained a mystery. Dutch and Hicks did not get along and Hicks was very jealous of any well that came in without his name on it. The news would get to Hicks soon and he would send his foreman and nephew, Darwin, to town to inspect the well and make sure it wasn't infringing on his drilling rights. A lot of the property Hicks had acquired he bought on a whim before Andrew McCracken's report was known about, and I now suspected Hicks wanted to cut his losses and capitalize on the knowledge to be found in that report.

Suddenly the batwing doors burst open and in walked Darwin followed by four seedy-looking bodyguards. He walked right up to Dutch and got in his face. "You struck oil on my claim, Dutch. I have a deed to that property right here in my hand."

The saloon went silent waiting for someone to speak.

"Your claim?" Dutch asked. "I thought you worked for Hicks."

"The claim is filed in Sacramento, Dutch, with Hicks' name on it," Darwin replied not addressing the slip up.

Dutch retorted, "Go to hell Darwin, go tell Hicks, his tricks won't work with me. Now you can either pull up a seat and have a drink or go out the way you came."

As Darwin considered his options the wildcatters and roughnecks from Henry's camp slowly crowded in around the two and Darwin could see he would get nowhere here. He took the drink, downed it, then grinned his ugly grin at Dutch. "We'll see whose claim stands up in court Dutch. Don't be spending any of my money."

Another slip. Darwin Anthony had been working for his uncle for twelve years. The Old Man was aging and his health seemed to be rapidly deteriorating. That Darwin would inherit everything was guaranteed; he'd made sure of that. Joseph Banks was Hicks' attorney, and had proven to be a bit impressionable.

As far as the title to the claim went, everyone knew that whoever owned Sacramento would own the claim. Both Dutch and his backers had politicians on their payroll in the state capital, as did Hicks. Hicks seemed to have dummy claims for every section of land in the area. His plan was to bully the real owners out of their land before they could call his bluff. Most of the smaller companies could not endure the costs of a prolonged court process, and they often would just walk away leaving their life savings on the table. As far as Dutch Henry was concerned, Darwin and Reynolds could bully him all they wanted. He possessed the presence of mind and the manpower to orchestrate and back up his own plans. Dutch recognized Reynolds as a cocky bully who seemed to get away with almost anything. Darwin on the other hand was a sly and thoughtful man who seemed to have a business mind much like his Uncle. He rarely came to town leaving most of the dirty work to Reynolds. Regardless, Dutch wasn't worried; he actually looked forward to the showdown in court.

While the laws were on the books, the judges would usually decide in favor of those who put money in their pockets. Since Hicks seemed to have most of the money, things would often go his way. I had a sneaky feeling though, that things were about to change. Somehow the death of Andrew McCracken and the arrival of McMann seemed to have turned the tides of the money flow.

I was up at 4:00 the next morning and made my way through the outskirts of town and arrived at the shack at exactly 5:00 am. McMann was already there apparently dropped off by Rex; the Packard was nowhere in sight. Lou arrived a bit later looking as dressed up as she could, considering the time and circumstances.

When she walked in both McMann and I stood as she settled herself into the third chair at the table.

"Thank you for coming, Miss Williams. My name is George M. McMann."

Lou looked shocked, not answering. She just sat there starring at McMann.

In an attempt to release the growing tension, I offered, "Lou, Mr. McMann works for Andrew McCracken's father. He is here to settle his estate and had a few questions I couldn't answer. He had asked for you, believing you could help him."

As if she didn't hear a word I said, Lou just looked straight at McMann and then asked in a very sharp tone, "Where did you come up with that name, mister?"

McMann sat quietly in his seat looking at Lou and then said in a mild tone, "Why Miss Williams you surprise me. One would think that you'd never heard that name before. John and Catherine gave you that name the day you were born. I'm surprised you have abandoned it so readily."

Now I understood. The fact that McMann had used her apparent last name, which no one this side of the Rockies had ever heard, was a bit much for Lou. McMann was good, he did his homework and didn't miss a thing.

"Look mister, I don't know who you are or what business you have digging into my past. What the hell do you want?"

"Miss Williams, Alex here has told me about your connection with Raymond Hicks, Darwin Anthony and Reynolds or Three-Finger Jack, whichever name he wishes to be carved on his tombstone. My concern is to find out who ordered Andrew McCracken killed and why. I believe you may have the information I need to settle this affair quickly. You see Miss Williams, the California climate does not agree with me. The heat and desert air give me hives, which make me very impatient and irritable."

After a short moment of silence he continued, "When you left Chicago all those years ago, your family was very worried. They sent out private investigators looking for you but you hid too well. I'm sorry to say that both your parents are dead now. It was a fire, they died in their sleep. Your sister Sadie is alive and lives on a little farm outside of Chicago. Her husband was killed in the war and her two sons have grown up. She lives alone."

I could see tears welling up in Lou's eyes. She had chosen a hard life. Why she left her home in Chicago, only she could know. It was obvious to me she had not thought of her family for many years and the thought of them now was devastating. McMann pulled a white silk handkerchief out of his pocket and handed it to her. She took it thankfully as a deep sob rolled through her body. McMann and I just sat there politely allowing her this reverie and reconnection to whom she once had been.

When she was ready, she told us in a quiet voice, "My real name was Sally. My sister, Sadie, was a couple years older than me and seemed to be the favorite of my father's. Pa, he never seemed to like me, and would beat me until I would go unconscious. My ma could do nothing. It started when I was about ten years old. He would come to me in the night and touch me. It scared me and I would resist and try to run away. When he caught me he would beat me and tell me I was a dirty little girl and no good. He said I belonged to the devil and did the devil's work.

"Finally one night when I was fifteen he came to me, I was waiting for him and I hit him over the head with a bottle. He kept coming, he beat me until I was almost dead. Sadie came to me and helped me escape. She took me to a friend's house and they hid me. When I recovered enough to walk, I ran away. I took some money Ma had hidden in the kitchen and caught a train out of town. I first went to Santa Fe, I worked at a restaurant there before coming to California. I liked San Francisco but one day I saw a man I recognized from back home. He had been a friend of my father's, and he was asking questions about me. My boss told me I better get out of town. She said this man had nothing good about him. I came here and settled into my profession. This town has been good to me, I like it here. It is the only home I've ever had."

We were silent; even McMann seemed a bit moved. I wondered about his background. What form of upbringing could create the person he had become? Perhaps he could relate to the abuse as a child. What would make a man so fastidiously neat but so ruthless in mind? I glanced at McMann. I felt sorry for him. I could feel the pain almost surface and noticed a slight reddening of his almost pure white complexion.

After what seemed like forever, McMann started again. "Sadie sends her love. She has asked that I give you this." He handed Lou a small broach. It was Scottish in nature. It had an inscription on it in Latin which read, "In Audrua Tendit." (I found out later it meant, "We attempt the heights.")

Calmly Lou accepted the broach and said, "It was my mother's. I always admired it and sometimes she would let me wear it. It came from her clan. Pa disapproved and insisted she not allow me to wear it. Sadie knew how much I loved it." She paused for a moment, then looked up at McMann's eyes, "How is she, is she well?"

The softness in McMann's eyes almost disturbed me, yet I was comforted to know this man did have a human side to him. What he did next further shocked me. He reached over and picked up her hands in his. His gestures were delicate and elegant. He held her hands, and as Lou looked up, McMann looked straight in her eyes and spoke. "Miss Williams, Sadie would like you to go to her. She is not well. The doctor says it is tuberculosis. She needs your help. There is a place in the desert, in New Mexico, that can help her. She needs you to accompany her there. Her sons have families of their own and can't take her. If you help me, help Mr. McCracken, and I find out who is ultimately responsible for Andrew's death, and you help us take him down, Mr. McCracken will provide the means for you and your sister to live out your lives together. He is a kind man and he loved his son very much. Andrew's death hit him hard. He has made a lot of money in his life and is growing old and getting tired. Before he dies, he will see to the downfall of Andrew's killer. He will spare no expense."

With that he was quiet, and he sat there holding Lou's hands, not moving a muscle. There seemed to be an enormous connection between McMann and Lou, understandably in how they so needed each other.

Finally Lou breathed a big sigh and said, "I will help you, Mr. McMann. I have lived an unsavory life. I have blamed my father for it, and for many years I even forgot I was ever a child. So you can understand that I have not thought about Sadie in many years. My sister Sadie was my only friend, and now I miss her. How can I get word to her?" Lou asked in a longingly disparate tone.

"I will send a message to her," McMann promised. "I will tell her I located you and that you will visit her soon. Right now we have work to do. Are you okay to continue?"

I wasn't sure what to expect. I had seen an amazing communication between two extreme personalities: Lou, the ever-resilient showgirl and lady of the evening, tough as rocks and clever as they come. And McMann, sly, conniving, treacherous, dangerous, and deadly, all contained in a petite, well-dressed package. Both came together in a moment so unpredictable and unprecedented that I was at a loss for words. They seemed to connect on some spiritual plane, which was untouchable to all but them. Now they were as one, even though cut from such different cloths. This was an amazing turn of events and I was very interested to see where the next few weeks would take this.

As I looked on, Lou seemed to transform right before my eyes. Now composed, she appeared to have come to some new resolve. She retracted her hands from those of McMann's and adjusted herself in her seat. She brushed back her hair and flipped her head back. Suddenly she was again, "The Lady Known as Lou."

"I will help you, Mr. McMann," she said. "If my sister needs me as you say, then let's finish this business so I can go to her. I know more about this town than you could imagine. When I was younger I was much sought after for my charm and looks, as well as ... I will leave the rest to your imagination. Men are weaklings, they think they come for sex, but it is more than that. They come for security and to feel loved. I provided that to many men in town.

"Often their wives are not forthcoming and men get anxious and even desperate for recognition of their needs, and for affection. They think they just come for a poke, but they need someone to talk to, someone who will listen. And let me tell you, they talked. And when they talked, I listened. And I remembered. I can tell you everything that has ever been told to me. I know every business deal that has happened and is going to happen and I know every shady businessman in town. If the information I have would get out, I could destroy almost anyone in town. Even the mayor, John Adams, has shared my pillow. Yes I am old, but I know how to make a man feel loved. They come to screw but they come for comfort and to feel for a moment in time, that they count for something. I will help you Mr. McMann, then you will take me to my sister. What do you want to know?"

I looked on with awe as this woman spelled it out. She was no fool and the image of an "aging prostitute" was replaced by that of an amazingly intelligent business woman. Even McMann seemed somewhat a bit in awe of her. I imagine he could relate to everything she said. When had he ever been loved? What of his mother? How had she sired a fellow such as George M. Mc-Mann? Had he ever been touched by a mother's love? Was he abandoned on a doorstep, orphaned at a young age, raised by some retched nun at a degraded orphanage? What was his story and what was it I was seeing in his eyes now?

We were interrupted by the door opening. Rex came in and said in a rather husky voice, "It is time, Mr. Mc-Mann."

McMann opened his watch, glanced at the time, and immediately transformed into Mr. George M. McMann, Esquire. He stood, brushed down his suit and then announced, "I have an appointment, Miss Williams. Thank you for meeting with me. I shall inform Mr. McCracken that you have agreed to help us. Mr. McCracken's personal physician will make a trip to

Chicago and see what he can do to help your sister.
Now I have a pressing engagement. Mr. McCoy will see
you safely back to town. Alex, you should know that I
have men in town. They will stay anonymous for now,
but they will protect both you and Miss Williams."

With that he and his man left. I sat there looking at
nothing particular, feeling a bit uncomfortable for both
myself and for Lou. What just happened was a very
personal and intimate encounter. I felt an intruder, as if
I was eavesdropping or invading their private lives.

Lou interrupted the silence by saying, "Well, Alex, I
guess this is it, the thing people talk about. That moment when your life becomes real. You either decide to
dive in or jump off. I have never backed up once in my
life so I guess I'm all in. This man, Mr. McMann, hit a
nerve with me. All that stuff about my family was
touching, but what I really got, was that this man believes in me. In a special way he got me. Few people
ever have. He knows what it is like to be me. Strangely
enough, I understand him as well. I would help him
regardless of what he could do for my sister. I feel him;
we are very similar at the core. I can't say I understand
it, but I know he will help me. He feels my pain and has
suffered my loss. One thing I can tell you, Alex, you are
on the right side. This man will not lose."

I dropped Lou off on Sixth Street, in a spot out of the
way and unfrequented by the populace.

Mac was in when I walked through the door.

"Up early I see," he said.

"That ain't the half of it," I replied. "I been up since four, hanging out with the most unlikely of allies." I proceeded to fill him in on the events of the morning. I'll give this to Mac, he took it all in and never doubted a word.

When I was done, he just looked at me and then picked up the phone. The next thing I knew, he had a man named Ralph Miller on the phone. He was the editor of the *Chicago Tribune*. Mac and Miller had a long association and were good friends.

Ralph had not heard of the Williams clan but would look into it. Mac asked him to look into the history of John and Catherine Williams and see if he could find any history. He mentioned Sadie and Sally and asked if he could find out anything at all.

Ralph said he would get back to Mac by tomorrow with whatever he found.

I had a quiet day at the office, by design. I cataloged everything that happened and sent a copy home for my ma to stow away in the shed. I could not believe everything that had transpired and couldn't help but think that I was a character in a dime novel mystery in some small oil town in the desert of central California.

A Day at the Courthouse

The next morning, Mac called me before I left the house and recommended I stop by the courthouse on my way in. When I got there, I encountered a huge crowd of roughnecks gathering in front. There was definitely a division among the troops.

On the left was Dutch Henry's group, and on the right was Jack Reynolds and a group of Hicks' mob.

It didn't take but a minute to figure out what this was all about. Darwin had filed suit against Dutch on Hicks' behalf regarding legal ownership of the property that the well had come in on, and Dutch was here to defend it.

Even though these disputes were commonplace regarding oil rights, it was often a legitimate argument between neighbors. In this case it was a turf war between Hicks and everyone who got in his way.

A small faction of bystanders was allowed into the courthouse and because I was press, I had a free ticket. Usually this would be a cut-'n-dry event, culminating in a quick decision. Today was a different story, and would set the stage for how the next few months would unfold.

Judge Harold Lindsey was presiding and William Mitchell was the bailiff who brought the court to order. Mitchell was a portly Englishman with a very thick mustache that culminated in thick bushy sideburns or muttonchops. His hair was parted down the middle and seemed glued to his head with grease. He stood about five feet, five inches tall and was about as wide. When he brought the court to order it was done as though he was introducing King George of England. When Judge Lindsey presented the case, an arbitrary and unexpected twist was introduced.

"Today, October 27th 1918, is case number 2927, involving a land owner dispute between three parties, Dutch Henry, Raymond Hicks, and Angus McCracken. The dispute will be determined based on the timely filing of the claim in our state's capital, or papers indicating the legal sale of such property preceding the moment of dispute therewith."

There was an immediate uproar among the audience amid basic confusion as to what was about to transpire. Banks, Hicks's attorney, immediately jumped up protesting the judge's action and demanded clarification. Darwin, who was present as well, stood, then realizing his mistake seated himself on the bench next to where Banks was standing. The judge acknowledged Bank's concern and so offered an explanation.

"The land known as the Old Rodriquez Estate, comprised of the section of land south of the coaling station, stretching south to Alexander Road then stretching west establishing one quarter section or 160 acres is in dispute.

"To clarify the contingency, it is understood that any claim to the property by Dutch Henry has been surrendered and turned over to Mr. Angus McCracken. Therefore, this hearing will proceed with the explicit purpose of determining ownership between Mr. Angus McCracken represented today by Mr. George M. McMann, Esquire, and one Raymond Hicks represented by Joseph Banks and Darwin Anthony." That Judge Lindsey left the title of "Esquire" off of his introduction of Banks did not go by unnoticed.

There was an immediate protest from Joseph Banks. He demanded the legitimacy of this statement and to this outrageous proposition. Judge Lindsey addressed Banks without precedence. "Mr. Banks, it is the understanding of the court that Dutch Henry sold all rights to the said claim to a Mr. Angus McCracken this morning for an undisclosed amount of money, and I have the papers here that were filed in the county clerk's office. Now, if there are no more interruptions, I will continue with this hearing to determine land ownership between Mr. McCracken, the apparent owner, and your client, Mr. Hicks, the plaintiff."

Banks, taken completely by surprise, could do nothing. Darwin, who had attended the hearing in jest more than by necessity, was dumbfounded. What under-handed turn of events had brought this about? The details had been planned and gone over. Judge Lindsey had understood the plan, had been given his marching orders, and all had agreed it was a slam dunk.

But in minutes, the court found in favor of Mr. McCracken, having found no valid evidence to the contrary. In fact, some documents which Banks presented were thrown out of court and labeled as suspect. Judge Lindsey gave Banks a warning regarding his techniques and suggested he should talk to his client, Mr. Hicks, about providing legitimate evidence in the future or face possible charges of fraud and contempt of court. Darwin tried to attract the attention of Lindsey but he was unsuccessful. Darwin was a dangerous man and had a temper to go with it. On Banks' insistence, Darwin refrained from saying anything, but was contemplating who would pay for this. The Old Man would be livid and that someone would be held accountable would go without saying.

Joseph Banks took his time getting to Hicks' ranch up in Priest Valley. He was not looking forward to the wrath of his employer when the Old Man found out about the judge's decision. Darwin decided to stay in town and see if he could come up with any information.

Banks found Hicks in his study looking at his library of books, none of which he had read. He liked to think himself a big man and had the books shipped in from

San Francisco for show. He may have opened one or two, but read them?

"What a waste of time it is to read," he would say to Darwin when he would thumb through the books. When Banks broke the news about the decision, it was a major blow. He rarely lost in court and because of his connections in Sacramento didn't expect to. Now by some unimaginable fluke not only did he lose a case, but he also lost a substantial piece of property which would produce millions of barrels of oil in the future.

Hicks was livid and decided he would take a rare trip into town to find out what the hell happened. He had a favorite old Model A and decided to crank it up and drive to town by himself.

A Meeting by Chance?

The judge was in his chambers as Hicks stormed in. "What the hell happened, Harry? This was all arranged; who screwed this up? I want them out of the picture now!" The judge, who was sitting at his desk, moved nothing except his eyes. Hicks followed his gaze only to see a small, well-dressed man, sitting comfortably in an overstuffed chair looking directly at him. His hands were folded in his lap and he looked almost like a porcelain doll.

"Who the hell are you, you scrawny bastard?" Hicks demanded without thinking. He had run this town since near the beginning, even if perhaps from the sly, but he was tired of these tenderfoots stepping on his toes. He'd had enough and on his way to town had decided to send those bastards out on a rail, tarred and feathered, if he had to.

McMann acted as if he hadn't heard him and sat rather relaxed in his chair. "I'm talking to you, punk, what are you doing in my town?" It was clear Hicks had let his guard down. Perhaps things had gone too well and too easy for too long. Hicks had acted like judge and jury when it came to the rule of law, and to date no one had challenged him.

The judge spoke up. "Mr. Hicks, meet Mr. George M. McMann, Esquire to Mr. Angus McCracken of South Carolina." Hicks, hearing the name was at first alarmed, but more annoyed in the end. "Fine, now, what the hell are you doing here and what makes you think you can swindle me out of what is rightfully mine?"

McMann slowly stood up, all five feet, two inches of him, and then addressed Hicks, "'Rightful' indeed Mr. Hicks. When it comes to rights, it seems my Sacramento politician trumps yours." McMann, left it at that waiting for what Hicks may do.

Hicks was not an educated man, not in schooling anyway, so the word "trumps" had him stumped.

"I don't know what the hell you are talking about, mister, but I think you are becoming very unpopular in my town. I suggest you find a ride out and take it."

"My client is Angus McCracken, his son Andrew was murdered here ten day ago. My boss sent me out here to settle his affairs. Mr. McCracken wasn't specific as to what that might mean, but I have been under his employ for quite some time and have a good understanding of his intentions. You see Mr. Hicks, Mr. McCracken has taken a sudden liking to the Coalinga oil fields. What he sees in it I have no idea. Personally, I can't stand the desert and the heat gives me hives, which makes me anxious. Regardless, he sent me out here and has authorized me to offer you 20 cents on the dollar for all your property and holdings. I took the liberty to have the papers drawn up."

McMann walked over to where Hicks was standing and held out a stack of papers. Hicks stood a good ten inches above McMann. "If you would please sign here and here, I can have the judge witness it and our business here will be done." McMann held out a pen pointing to the place the signatures should be placed.

Hicks was completely caught off guard. He stared at the papers in McMann's hand then made a guttural sound as he reared back and swung his melon sized fist at McMann's same-sized head. McMann simply ducked, not making a big deal about it, placed his left leg behind Hicks' right and gave a gentle shove. Hicks lost his balance and toppled over before he knew what happened. McMann moved in such a way that all one would see was Hicks' swinging and falling and nothing from McMann.

McMann extended a hand saying, "Excuse me, Mr. Hicks, you must have tripped. Can I give you a hand up?" Hicks accepted it, not quite sure what just happened.

Judge Lindsey leaned back in his overstuffed leather chair and put both arms behind his head, thoroughly enjoying the show. Hicks had threatened Lindsey on many occasions and had ramrodded him into legal decisions that were not always legitimate. Lindsey loathed Hicks and was very happy to have finally been able to rule against him. It was clear that McMann was a man to be reckoned with.

Lindsey had gotten a background check done on McMann and learned that his ties went back as far as the founding of the country and maybe even further. The search ended there as his source had found that there were dead ends to his inquiries. He had said to Lindsey, "I'm sorry, Harry. I don't have access to that information. All I know is that his connections and his power run deep."

McMann was an enigma, and it appeared that Coalinga was ripe for an all-out turf war.

Hicks got up and seemed to be trying to think clearly. It seemed there was nothing he could do to bully his way out of this, to use his hit men seemed inappropriate or ineffective for this kind of battle. No, he was going to have to think on this, but he knew he would figure it out.

Hicks looked over at McMann who seemed impervious to everything, as he was calmly arranging the papers on a table in the corner of the room. McMann saw the opportunity and addressed Hicks. "Mr. Hicks, it would be in your best interest to sign these papers, take your profits and find some hole to crawl into. You are through here. Mr. McCracken is prepared to offer you

$500,000 for all of your oil holdings, all 3,553 head of your cattle, and the 20,000-acre Priest Valley Ranch. He also will offer you $50,000 for your interest in the cannery in Monterey. But I must warn you, Mr. Hicks, this offer is only valid as we speak. If you don't sign these papers in the next..." McMann paused and took his watch out of his vest, pushed the stem to open the cover and studied it briefly, "...five minutes, the deal is off of the table. I'd advise you to take the offer, Mr. Hicks. You cannot win here."

McMann closed his watch and slowly placed it back in his pocket while holding the gaze of an apparently hobbled Raymond Hicks.

Hicks just stood there with his mouth slightly open. While $500,000 was a lot of money, his holdings in the oil fields would yield millions within the next five years. But more of a concern was how did McMann know so much about his holdings – the number of cattle, which was accurate, and even about his share in the cannery in Monterey? That information was hidden so well from public record that he couldn't understand it… unless Banks had said something. Banks, his image burned in Hicks' mind. Yes, of course, he knew he shouldn't trust that money-grubbing galoot. He was now sure that Banks had betrayed him. Hicks was already thinking about what he would do, how he would make Banks pay for this.

His thoughts were interrupted by the words of Judge Lindsey. "Mr. Hicks, what is your decision? I have other business this afternoon and must clear my quarters. If you wish to take Mr. McCracken's offer, I will witness the signing and we can all be on our way." Lindsey knew Hicks wouldn't sign it, he was too stupid to see that he was beaten. Lindsey had seen this kind of play before back in Washington. He didn't have to know any more about McMann or McCracken, he could see the power play behind the move. McCracken would go to no end to crush the man responsible for the death of his only son. Lindsey could see the cleverness in the money offer, just enough to spark an interest, yet not enough to squelch Hicks' greed. McCracken knew Hicks would reject his offer and he knew that McMann knew just what to do to squeeze Hicks until he popped. Lindsey was going to enjoy this.

Hicks threw up his hands and said, "You tell your boss to go to hell. You know as well as I that this land is worth millions, millions. I own more land in this damn valley than the rest of the town all together. It's mine. I've earned it and I'll be damned if I will let a small-town pipsqueak attorney and his master swindle me out of what is rightfully mine. You go to hell, all of you!" With that he stormed out of the judge's chambers, leaving a vacuum of silence as he went.

McMann, while collecting his papers, looked up at Judge Lindsey and said, "I guess I will be residing at the International for a few more days. Good day, your Honor." With that he simply walked out of the room.

Judge Lindsey just sat in his chair unable to think clearly. He reached over to the mother of pearl inlaid box on his desk, opened it and extracted a fine cigar, bit off the end, struck a match, and sucked the hot flame into the fine tobacco. After a minute he sat back, put his feet on his desk and smiled.

A Bottle of Whiskey

Hicks stood on the steps of the courthouse gazing at nothing in particular. Whatever had just happened in the judge's chambers had not really sunk in, but he knew he had to think fast or everything he had worked for over the years would be lost. McCracken seemed like such an easy target; the Old Man hadn't considered who he really was. This had been a mistake he usually never made. Was he slipping?

Shortly, McMann exited the building with a black satchel under his arm. Hicks looked on as the pathetic little man walked past him as though he wasn't there, down the steps then across the street to the International. Hicks had the urge to go squash the man right there. How dare this porcelain rat threaten his world and all he had worked so hard for?

Something was different with this man though, and Hicks had some figuring to do. He decided to do something he rarely did; he decided to walk down to Fifth Street and have a drink. After that he'd visit Lou, for she'd know how to settle his nerves.

The Riggins was full up when Hicks entered the place. Many of the inhabitants were men from his own company. When he was recognized, the room got very quiet. As Hicks made his way across the crowded room to the bar, a path opened up as if Moses was parting the Red Sea. Nobody wanted to get in his way and everybody felt a chill as he passed. Many men had never actually seen Raymond Hicks; they only knew him by reputation. That he was in the Riggins today after the decision by Judge Lindsey was a very curious thing.

After the court hearing, word of the outcome had spread through town like a wildfire. By the time Joseph Banks had returned to the Priest Valley Ranch and related the news to Hicks, every roughneck in every bar and saloon in town was talking about it. Several fights had broken out between Hicks' roughnecks and other company crews as comments were made. One man lay dead from a knife piercing his lung. Several others were nursing bruises and cuts. As with most brawls on Fifth Street, after the initial upset and explosion of emotions wore out, anyone who was able to would go back to drinking, forgetting what started the argument in the first place. The body of the dead man was carried to the back door to await the undertaker and his rig. He would usually make his rounds once a day collecting the less fortunate victims of Fifth Street.

"What will you have, Mr. Hicks?" the bartender asked.

"Whisky," Hicks replied. "I'll take a bottle." Hicks downed a shot allowing the fiery liquid to roll down

the back of his throat. He turned his gaze to the back of
the room spying a table where he could get lost in his
thoughts. As he moved toward the back of the room,
again a path opened up before him. When he reached
the table he wanted, he just stood there looking at the
men occupying it. Within seconds the men compre-
hended the message and disappeared almost as quickly
as the roaches that frequented the kitchen.

Hicks sat and contemplated the bottle. What had gone
wrong? He had planned this very well. McCracken
would be killed, Reynolds would find the report with
McCracken's recommended drilling sites and the best
properties. Hicks would acquire McCracken's land,
which undoubtedly would yield millions in oil. He
would become the King of Coalinga's oil fields.

Hicks considered his options. For the past 30 years he
had systematically purchased sections of land in the
Coalinga corridor. He owned several thousand acres
and exercised mineral rights on all of them. In the early
days, before Ford created the assembly line of automo-
biles, oil was not so valuable. But now, with the auto-
mobile revolution, oil was in high demand. Many large
corporations were beginning to buy up the little man or
drive him out of business. It was imperative that he
acquire substantial holdings or he might, and probably
would, fall to the giants emerging in the industry.

The time was right to strike. If he didn't move fast, he
and his holdings would be swept up in the abyss. Perhaps he should have taken McCracken's offer. The hell

with it, no Johnny-come-lately rebel was going to get what he had worked so hard for. To hell with McCracken and Mr. George M. McMann. He would show them a thing or two.

His thoughts went to his nephew, Darwin Anthony. He was his sister's son. When she was killed in the San Francisco earthquake back in '06, Darwin had sought Hicks out, remembering that his ma had talked about her no-account brother, as Darwin would relate. Darwin and his sidekick, Jack Reynolds, had shown up at his ranch about three weeks after the quake. Raymond Hicks had never married, and was kind of liking the idea of family. The fact that Darwin was streetwise and afraid of nothing was a plus. Reynolds seemed to have no conscience which could be even more valuable.

Hicks had groomed these kids to be his soldiers. They could fight, steal, con any man, and they had proved equally able to kill without question. They proved a huge asset to Hicks. He felt no remorse himself for eliminating distractions from his goal (no matter what their name might be), but was just as happy to have someone to do his dirty work for him.

The oil fields were tough territorial holds. Almost any day, gunshots would drive roughnecks into hiding. Many times shots were fired back and forth just to keep the peace. Occasionally someone would get nicked but rarely killed. Most of the battles took place in the saloons at night, where crews fought other crews over such things as who worked faster, better, smarter.

These comments would set the barroom floor on fire and oftentimes two to three bodies would be all that was ultimately produced from it all.

Hicks drank in peace and considered the crowd as well as his options. He would talk to Darwin. Darwin understood him and ultimately would run the business as Hicks slowed down. As he thought about this, a coughing spree overcame him, and he coughed uncontrollably until blood was more prevalent than the sputum. He considered this. Whatever was affecting his lungs was not easing up at all. He had caught a cold two years ago and hadn't been able to shake it. He was spending more time in his library, looking at all the books he'd never read. Maybe he should try reading one. Naaa! Why start now?

Hicks was so deep in contemplation that he didn't hear the fighting begin until the gunshots rang out. He was quickly alert to the situation and dove under the table. This had been his trained response to danger, one he wasn't necessarily proud of, but it proved to have staying power.

When the dust settled, Reynolds stood over the body of a known Dutch Henry wildcatter. Darwin suddenly appeared standing at Hicks' table yielding a sawed-off shotgun. Nobody was moving. "Come on, Unc, it's time to go home," Darwin addressed Hicks. Without a word, Hicks shot off his last drink and Darwin helped him up. With Reynolds holding his 1911 Colt and Darwin wielding the widow-maker, the three backed out of the saloon, flanked by some 35 roughnecks employed under the Hicks brand.

"What were you thinking, Uncle, going into that saloon alone? You could have been killed and probably would have if Reynolds hadn't stepped in. That man he killed had a derringer in his hand and was sighting you in. You're getting old Uncle, I don't think you are thinking clearly. Let me take you home."

Hicks, somewhat affected by the contents of the bottle now inside of him had no good argument. Darwin rolled Hicks into the Model A as Reynolds cranked it over, and Darwin started for their home in Priest Valley. Reynolds agreed to stay in town and pick up any information he could. His specialty.

From the Beginning

As Darwin turned down Main Street starting the hour ride home, he noticed his uncle had passed out from all the liquor he had consumed. Darwin started thinking about his life, his future and his past.

Everything had played out very well for him in his life, ever since the quake in '06. He was 14 when it hit. He'd lived with his ma, Hicks' sister, in a shanty near the waterfront on the east side. She was a poor widow whose husband had died on San Juan Hill, trying to reach the top with Teddy Roosevelt.

"He was a fool," she would say, "running away to fight in a war, thinking life would be easier there, than it would be raising a bratty little kid while working on the waterfront. I should have never allowed myself to get pregnant," she said. "I thought having you would keep him here, but instead you just made him run faster and farther. Now I'm stuck in this little shack with no one but a little brat to feed. You get out Darwin, go make some money so we can eat tonight. Don't come back empty handed or I'll whip you till you're dead."

The first shock of the earthquake had knocked him off his feet and back against the wall. He seemed to be thrown back and forth, tossing and turning. He heard a bloodcurdling scream from his mother, which stopped suddenly amid the rumbling and crashing that engulfed them. There was a deep and ominous roar from somewhere near the center of the earth, and it twisted and contorted the little shack in which Darwin lay.

The second shock seemed more powerful than the first and as Darwin hunkered down, he felt for and found his mom. He recalled the second wave continuing to rock the world up and down like a violently shaken carpet. It was about five o'clock in the morning. The roaring, swaying, and grinding hit with a tremendous force and seemed to continue for a long time. And then when it stopped, there was an eerie silence. Darwin recalled lying on the floor holding onto his ma's leg, shaken and afraid, wondering what or who had been hitting him and hoping it would stop. He laid there with his eyes shut tight, afraid of what he would see if he opened them. He just lay there waiting for his ma to say something. She never did. She never moved. When Darwin had recovered enough courage to open his eyes and look up, all he saw was the pile of bricks, which had once been their chimney, piled up in front of him. It engulfed what was left of his mother. He let go of her lifeless leg and crawled backward until he felt his way blocked by a wall. He remembered just pulling his knees to his chest and rocking back and forth, back and forth. Suddenly a third shock hit. The weakened walls began to crumble and topple as he scrambled as fast as he could to get out of what was left of the building. It collapsed with a final roar behind him. He never looked back.

People were running everywhere; men, women, and children, all running wild or walking in a daze. He saw a woman carrying the body of her lifeless child. Some men were helping others as they limped or crawled to safety as they scrambled amongst the rubble. Residents of his small community lay either dead or wounded in the streets. He recalled the chaos that ensued.

Suddenly all his senses were alert. There was an angry yell followed by a gunshot. He saw a man fall flat on his face not ten feet in front of him. Blood poured from his neck darkening the sandy road. Before he knew it, the shooter stood over the dead man then ripped a satchel out of his lifeless hand. He briefly looked up into Darwin's frightened eyes before running up the street disappearing into a crowd of pandemonium.

Darwin studied the body in front of him, he'd never seen a dead man before, and the contorted lifeless body etched an image in his mind. He saw his father in this fellow, useless and spent. He didn't know what made him do it, but his next actions were the defining moments in Darwin's life. With no sign of emotion or remorse, Darwin moved over to the body of the dead man. He turned him over and started going through his pockets. He found a gold watch, a sack containing coins, a small gun which he recalled was a derringer with some extra bullets. In the top pocket of his jacket he found a wad of bills, the stack was about an inch thick. As he stuck the money deep in his pocket and stood, he noticed the face of the dead man. His eyes were open seemingly staring directly into those of Darwin's. They were empty, hollow, devoid of all that he had been.

There was another aftershock which shook Darwin out of the trance those eyes had fixed upon him. Suddenly he began to run. As he made his way through the rubble which was once San Francisco, he began to notice a freedom in his soul. He felt excitement; there was nothing to hold him back, no one to tell him what to do. He was 14 years old and he felt like his life had just begun. He had hated his ma; she only ever beat him and told him how he ruined her life. She lived to drink and drink she did. There were men that would visit her. They would drink and laugh and disappear behind the curtain defining her bedroom.

Darwin hated them for he would have to leave the house and wander the street along the waterfront. He could remember his pa, a quiet man who never really said much to Darwin; he just come home late after working and drinking at some bar. Ma would see him coming and they would fight until Darwin fell asleep and probably later. When the boy woke up the next morning his pa was gone again and his ma usually had a new bruise or cut on her face. Darwin had learned to leave the house early before his ma could give him one of his own to match hers.

Sticking close to the waterfront he worked his way to the barrio. He had a hideout there, which would provide him some protection, if it still stood. He encountered many obstacles along the way. Not only were the streets blocked in many areas with rubble and fire, but everywhere he looked there were people wandering, fighting, and looting. He had just turned up an alley, which would lead him to his hideout, when he was confronted by a bigger kid he knew. Louie was not a nice boy and on many occasions had beaten Darwin and stolen anything he had in his possession. This time Louie had blood on his shirt and a wild look in his eye. He looked at Darwin and came for him. "You're a dead man, Darwin!" he said as he raised a club he was holding ready to strike Darwin down. He didn't realize, and wouldn't in another second, that Darwin was holding the derringer. The smaller boy just pulled it out of his pocket and shot Louie right between the eyes. Louie just stood there wobbling on his feet. He dropped the club before falling forward, flat on his face.

Darwin walked over to the limp body, which had been Louie and turned him over. There were those same eyes he had seen earlier staring up at him, lifeless, empty, and alone. Darwin rifled through his pockets finding some money, both paper and coins, a watch and some gold jewelry. He put it in his pocket and was about to continue forward when he heard the faint whimpering of a child in the bushes close by.

Holding onto the derringer he ventured a look behind the bushes. There to his surprise was a bloody but alive kid he'd known from the neighborhood. He was a couple years younger than Darwin but he recognized him. He wasn't sure why he did it, but Darwin put out a hand and told the kid to come with him.

When he located what was left of his hiding place, he led the kid inside and they both sat against the wall of the old building and said nothing. Minutes passed before Darwin spoke. "What happened to your pa, Jack?"

"I think he got killed," Jack replied. "The house just collapsed and when I tried to go inside, there was no place to go, it was just flattened. Old Man Kelley told me to get as far away as I could. He told me that I would have to make it on my own. Dar, if you hadn't of come along when you did, I think Louie would have killed me. He was enjoying hitting me with that club. He'd hit me and then ask if it hurt. I kept saying no because I didn't want him to feel like he'd got the best of me. I hated him, it's good he's gone, Dar."

Darwin sat in silence, taking in the situation, feeling nothing, no sympathy for the fallen Louie.

That day was the beginning of an alliance, which would last for the next several years. Jack Reynolds owed his life to Darwin Anthony and he would spend the rest of his days trying to earn Darwin's trust. He would continue this quest until the day that he died.

The city was ablaze and in ruin, but for Darwin and Jack, it was a land of opportunity. Both boys had grown up to this point streetwise and crafted in the art of pickpocketing and the like. Darwin already had a good wad of cash in his possession, but felt it necessary to add to his coffers.

There were looters everywhere, but oftentimes they would be shot on sight. Or maybe there would be a judge, jury, and semblance of a trial, and then the sentence would be rendered through the barrel of a Colt .45, .38 special or a sawed-off shotgun.

Darwin and Jack had an easier time of it, being "poor starving kids, orphaned victims of the disaster," they had doors opened to then which landed them in the "land of opportunity," giving them the keys to the city.

Jack, being smaller, almost scrawny, would limp into a camp of refugees and create a distraction with tears exploiting the beating that Louis had given him, while Darwin would make a quick survey of the inhabitants' possessions. Most of the refugees in the camps had collected many of their valuables before fleeing their homes. They were ripe for the picking. Darwin focused on the small things, mostly money and jewelry, things that could be easily hidden in pockets.

As things settled out in the weeks that followed, the confusion became less and the boys' schemes became less effective. Ultimately, finally being discovered in the act, Darwin was almost killed by a young woman yielding a pistol. With that the boys gathered their spoils and headed for the hills.

Heading south out of town, they kept to the shadows, ducking in and out of fallen structures, aware that there were others with minds like theirs. They were determined they would not fall prey to thieves like themselves. On the third day, Jack discovered an old horse stranded in a corral. It appeared that the horse had been there since the quake had hit, apparently abandoned by his owner. The horse seemed genuinely glad to see them. The boys found some grain in the fallen barn and enough water for the horse to wash it down with. As they watched the horse fill his stomach, perhaps for the first time in days, they rested in the soothing warmth of the sun while sitting on the top rail of the corral gate.

Darwin recalled the dream-like feeling he had at that moment. It was as if he had awoken from a terrible nightmare, which had actually been his life. Jack sat next to him saying nothing. Their reverie was interrupted by the probing muzzle of their newfound friend. As the horse approached them, he seemed to be investigating their intentions, smell, and character. Neither boy had ever touched a horse before. Oh, they'd run from them as the constable rider would chase them from the better part of town, but as they touched the softness and smoothness of the horse's nose, face, and neck, they sensed a grateful curiosity, a thankfulness from the beast.

The horse's nostrils flared as great volumes of wind traveled to and from his nose as he tested the air's message. As the boys sat on the rail the horse pushed his way forward enjoying their company. He made a nickering sound, which made them laugh, and the horse stood there pushing at the boys with his huge head. They noticed his strange eyes, that one was blue and one was brown did not get past them. For the first time in weeks and possibly for the first time ever for the boys, they felt safe. The big horse gave them comfort, and as they sat there taking in each other, they felt an amazing bond form between them, and at that moment, a partnership was formed.

They named the horse Willy. Jack produced a bridal he found in the dilapidated barn. Not knowing what to do with it, they were relieved that Willy accepted the bit willingly. They'd seen the police horses enough to get the idea of what it looked like on the horse's head, and they finally figured out how to get the leather straps over the horse's ears and fastened around its neck. Next, they climbed up the corral gate and chanced climbing up on Willy's back. To their surprise and great relief, Willy seemed genuinely pleased to have them aboard. They pushed the gate open and not knowing how to steer the thing, gave Willy his head.

Willy seemed to want to get as far away from the city as possible. The smoke and ashes were uninviting and the stench of decay was beginning to permeate the area. They traveled all day meandering up through the redwoods then towards the coolness of the coast. The boys seemed content to just have a place to sit even if it was on the horse's back, and soon the three fell into a rhythm all their own.

They spent the first night camping by a small stream, which found its way down the mountain eventually colliding and blending with the shoreline. There was a nice grassy glen sided by tall redwoods, which provided shelter from the wind. Willy stood close by, standing watch. His tail warding off the pesky flies, as he stood with his ears forward and nostrils flared, alert to any potential dangers in the surrounding environment. Darwin observed the attentiveness of the large animal and was both fascinated and comforted by his attentiveness. The boys snacked on the last bits of food they had stored in the old burlap sack they carried with them, and then eventually fell asleep nestled amongst the redwood sorrel and fallen trees.

By nightfall of the second day, they found themselves approaching a small fishing village on the coast. There were dilapidated shacks along the way, but they continued on and soon found the village. They were mostly Portuguese fishermen, but there was a faction of Chinese as well. The boys were welcomed and offered food and warmth. They stayed for two days resting and eating their fill.

About this time Darwin began to recall that his ma had a brother who lived down south. He couldn't remember meeting him, but thought it was a good idea to at least try to find him. Jack having no other relatives he knew of, agreed.

On the morning of the third day, they bid their hosts goodbye and headed south. Their hosts provided them with a sack of food and some blankets. They mentioned that the town of Santa Cruz was a two- to three-day ride, so off they went. There was a trail hugging the ridge, which was the one they chose to follow. One of the Portuguese fellows had warned them of bandits along the coast road and suggested they stay out of sight.

Neither of the boys had ever been out of the city, and the experience of riding among and below the giant redwoods was something neither would ever forget. The solitude and stillness of the woods was comforting and they rode on with the only sound being that of Willy's hooves kicking the trail and the occasional sound of a far off bird, who's eerie cadence echoed off and away through the forest.

They camped that night by another small stream, which flowed into the ocean. They decided to stay away from the farmhouse they discovered, and camped again in a small glen surrounded by redwoods. It was beautifully set among the forest and the gentle rippling water lulled them to sleep.

On the Wharf in Santa Cruz

When they reached the outskirts of Santa Cruz on the morning of the fourth day, they sat on Willy, overlooking the bustling town.

Darwin decided their best bet was to ride into town and tell the authorities that they were victims of the quake and that they were brothers. He would tell them that their mother had sent them south to meet up with their uncle, a Raymond Hicks, who owned a ranch down south. He was right in thinking that if they were discovered to be orphans, they would have been detained and become wards of the state. Both Darwin and Jack knew of this because of some of the boys they had known living in the barrio of San Francisco. These were boys who had escaped from the ill-fated confines of the wards, and were living freely on the street.

That Darwin could produce a pittance of money, "which his ma gave him," helped their story. When they found the sheriff and wove their yarn, he bought it hook, line, and sinker. The boys were already both excellent con artists and put on the perfect good little boy act. The story was that Darwin, being the older brother, was in charge of seeing to it that they made it to their uncle's. Their mother would meet them there as soon as she settled her affairs in San Francisco.

The sheriff pointed out a general store where Darwin purchased a new set of clothes for the both of them. He also bought some bedrolls and a hat for each of them. They ate at a little café on the wharf called Gilda's. The people were very nice, and the older Italian lady doted on little Jack so much that he turned red in the face.

As they were finishing their lunch, the sheriff showed up with some good news. He had located the where-abouts of Raymond Hicks. He owned a large cattle ranch south of Monterey called the Double Bar 7, it was only a four- or five-day ride south. It was good that Darwin remembered his uncle's name. The fact that he was a known rancher and landowner gave credence to their story, authenticating their journey. Otherwise the Sheriff could easily have detained the two stray boys until a proper solution could be rendered.

Because Darwin and Jack acted like well-behaved children (and how they knew what that looked like, was beyond Darwin, now as he was reminiscing), the sheriff was willing to trust their story.

Not wanting to push their luck, they headed south out of town early the next day. The Sheriff had actually provided a map as well as a letter of passage they could show to any suspicious inquirers along the way.

Priest Valley

Four days later they crested the ridge that would lead them into Priest Valley and to the Double Bar 7. The vastness of the scenery which confronted them was arresting. The rolling grass covered hills seemed to go on forever. Darwin remembered wondering how far they went and who owned them. As they rode on, they started seeing small groups of cattle grazing on the land. When they descended a forested trail which opened up into a wide valley, they knew that they had arrived.

Off at the end of the meadow was a grove of large oaks, and nestled among and beneath them was a large ranch-style house. There were several barns and what appeared to be a long bunkhouse. They could hear the distinct "plink, plink, plink" of steel on an anvil and recognized the sound of a blacksmith working on some project. There was the sound of roosters challenging the wind and faint voices and laughter of men working around the place.

After a few minutes of silent awe, Darwin told Jack it was time to go in and meet their destiny. They started Willy toward the ranch house. Willy, sensing their tension, rode forward with the intention of bolting at the first sign of trouble. He held his head high, his ears pointed forward and his nostrils flared. In the few days that they established their friendship, Willy had come to think of himself as the leader of the herd. The three were on their own and survival was their game.

As they approached the farmhouse, the sound of their approach was signaled by the bark of a lazy old hound dog, who didn't even bother to get up to greet them. He just lay in the shade of an old oak tree and howled their announcement. All motion around the ranch stopped as all eyes looked upon the two approaching boys mounted on top of an old horse.

Darwin stopped Willy a ways out and the two boys just sat there on Willy with their hearts pounding inside their rib cage. Willy stood perfectly still breathing through wide nostrils, taking in what information the wind would tell him.

Presently, a big door opened on the main house and a rather large and well-weathered man appeared and walked out on the porch. He wore a sidearm and held a Winchester Rifle in the crook of his right arm. When he recognized the intruders as mere boys, his hardened face lightened a bit. He placed the rifle against the side of the house and stepped down off the porch and approached the visitors.

Darwin was scared to death as was Jack. Darwin held the derringer in his hand concealed in his pocket and waited as the man approached.

"Well I'll be damned," Hicks started. "Who the hell are you two varmints and what makes you think you can just ride in here trespassing on my land?"

"My name is Darwin Anthony, my ma was your sister. She died in the quake, and I ain't got no place to go. She told me about you before, so when that chimney fell on her leaving her dead, I figured I'd come find you and see what I could do to earn a living here."

Darwin was so nervous he just kept on talking. "Jack here, his dad was squashed under a building and he ain't got nobody but me to keep him fed. We are hard workers and just want a place to alight and set a few days. If we don't cut the mustard, you can send us a-packin'."

With that, he shut up. There was a moment of silence and then an explosion of laughter from Hicks.

"You boys come on down off that nag and come set a bit. Cookie's got some stew a-brewin' and I need some likely guinea-pigs to make sure it ain't poison. He's been trying to kill me for nearly 20 years with that cooking of his, but I'm still a-livin'. Thank god for all the varmints that come a-visitin'.

As Darwin and Jack got down off of Willy, an old man walked up and took the reins. "What'cha you want me to do with this old nag, boss?" he addressed Hicks. "If it don't eat, send it to the glue factory," Hicks replied.

Darwin stopped short, pulled out his derringer pointing it right at the old man saying, "Mister, you do anything other than feed and water my horse, I'll kill you."

Judd looked up at the barrel of that derringer and let out a big belly laugh. "Kid, I been shot at and hit with bullets from guns a lot bigger than that. That little pea shooter of yours ain't got enough poop to pierce my hide. Relax son, I was just a-jossin'. Put that thing away before somebody gets hurt."

Hicks was standing there observing the whole thing, liking what he saw. He led the boys into the ranch house, which was larger than any other house either Darwin or Jack had ever been in. It was spacious, filled mostly with well-made handcrafted oak furniture, much of it covered with cowhide. Darwin heard Jack stop short and turned to see him starring at a large bear skin laying on the floor acting as a rug. The bear's head was facing the door, with his mouth, which was full of large teeth, wide open as if looking for something to chew on.

Hicks noticed the boy's concern and let out a large roar which made them both jump. He let out another belly laugh and said, "Come on boys, that there bear's kid-eatin' days are over."

Then he disappeared around the corner, which led to the eating table in the kitchen. Cookie was an old

Chinaman dressed in his traditional clothing. Darwin and Jack were used to this attire from visiting the Chinese town in San Francisco.

"Slop up some of that poison for these here boys to try Cookie. I don't want to get killed today by your cooking so I brought in these greenhorns to do the dying for me."

Cookie said some words in Chinese that no one, not even Hicks could decipher, but the intent was clearly understood.

Cookie dished up the slop and brought two bowls to the boys who sat sheepishly at the table. Darwin was beginning to wonder if it was a good idea to look up his uncle after all. He felt a bit better when Hicks pulled up a chair and Cookie brought him a bowl from the same pot. Regardless, the boy hesitated to eat until Hicks filled his mouth a couple of times. The stew was some of the best food either boy had ever eaten. It was rich with beef and filled with garden vegetables. They emptied their bowls and accepted a refill from Cookie.

Hicks finished his meal and pushed his bowl across the table. Cookie was quick to recover it and carry it to the kitchen.

Hicks rolled himself a smoke then offered the makings to the two boys. Neither knew what to do with it so they passed. Hicks lit his smoke then addressed Darwin straight out.

"So, Rachel's dead, is she?"

When Darwin explained the events of her death, Hicks just sat there and listened, not saying a word. "That no account husband of hers still alive?" he asked.

Darwin had to inform him of the fact that his pa had died seven years ago on San Juan Hill. He told Hicks his pa was some kind of hero. "Hero!" Hicks barked. "If I know'd your pa, and I did, Old Teddy probably shot him for desertion. He was good for nothing. I tried to get your ma away from him, but she was smitten. Your ma never had no sense anyhow. Well, I'm sorry she is gone. We were never very friendly to each other. I was away on my own by the time she was knee high to a grasshopper."

"Where'd you get that pea shooter, boy? Let me see it."

"I just come by it," Darwin remarked, "and I ain't about to turn it over to nobody. I ain't no greenhorn."

Hicks looked down at the boy with a furrowed brow, intimidation his intent. When Darwin held his ground and didn't budge, Hicks looked on with some kind of respect. This kid was right, he wasn't no greenhorn. Hicks decided then and there he would take the kid in under his wing and raise him as the son he'd never had.

"What of you, boy?" He addressed Jack. "What is your story?"

"I ain't got no story yet, mister. I plan on making it up as I go."

Even Darwin was impressed with his answer. Darwin always liked Jack. He was small but never let anybody make him back up. He would take anything that come his way. Once when Darwin asked him why he took it and didn't run, Jack looked up at him through his blooded nose and blackened eyes and said, "Nothing's killed me yet, Darwin, and until it does, I ain't a-planning to move anywhere but forward."

That was 16 years ago and the truth is, he'd never seen Jack back up from any situation, no matter how unfavorable the odds may seem.

Hicks had to respect the kid, red-haired, freckled, and a bit of a crazed look in his eye. As he watched Jack scrape the last bits of broth from his bowl, he noticed that Jack was missing the lion share of the pinky on his right hand.

"Where'd you lose that finger boy?" Hicks asked. Jack just looked up at Hicks with meanness in his eyes, then after a moment said, "Lost it in Chinese Town." That was all that he'd let out. Even Darwin didn't know the whole story about the incident until years later.

Hicks looked down at Jack and saw no back up in the boy. "You'll do, son, you'll do. You boys can stay on. You will work for your room and board and I'll pay you a fair wage beyond that. If I ever catch you steeling or lagging on your chores or responsibilities, you better run faster than I can shoot or we'll be buryin' you in a shallow grave up there on boot hill."

That was the beginning of Darwin's association with his Uncle Ray and the beginning of a long and profitable relationship between Hicks and the two boys.

How Three-Finger Jack
Became Two-Finger Jack

Reynolds stayed at the Riggins after Darwin and Hicks headed home, to make sure the consensus was that his was a fair fight. It was apparent that the dead man was none other than the wildcatter, Dry-Hole Charlie. Charlie certainly had motive and he did have a gun in his possession. Whether it was truly his or whether Reynolds somehow planted it on him was unimportant at this point. It couldn't be proven one way or the other, so the event would just be swept under the carpet as so many other killings had been. I began to wonder that if Reynolds were to notch his gun as in the days of the old west, if there would be anything left of its stock.

Dry-Hole Charlie was a well-known wildcatter in the oil industry. Until he struck it big with Dutch and his last well, every hole he spudded in came up dry. That the claim to his only successful dig was somehow challenged by Hicks, was motive enough for a killing. Hicks' crew had a history of several run-ins with Dry-

Hole Charlie and it was well known that there was no love lost between Dry-Hole and Reynolds. The fact that Mr. Angus McCracken ended up with the claim was irrelevant.

After the shooting, Reynolds bellied up to the bar and ordered a bottle of his favorite drink, tequila. There was quite a commotion about Charlie's death among the different factions, and they were each keeping to the security of their own corners of the saloon. Dry-Hole, although lousy at picking spots for spudding-in that produced, was generally well liked among the rough-necks. It was apparent that the stability of the Coalinga oil fields was about to crack.

Reynolds continued to work his way through his bottle and although surrounded by men that would be his antagonists, there was a respectable distance between him and the next man. When Reynolds got to drinking, no man was safe, nor woman for that matter.

In the years that had passed since Jack and Darwin first appeared at the Double Bar 7, each had developed into their respective roles and personalities. Darwin had become the heir apparent, taking on the role of adopted son and apprentice to Hicks, while Three-Finger Jack Reynolds became the "enforcer" you might say. He had no conscience that was apparent, and seemed to have the unnerving ability to appear and disappear as if by magic. He was the guy that always made you feel like you were being watched or followed. It was suspected by those honest citizens of Coalinga, and rightly so, that much of the strong-arming by, and positioning in, the Hicks organization, was the responsibility and orchestration of Three-Finger Jack Reynolds. Regardless, no crime could ever be linked to him, and any circumstantial evidence, if it existed at all, was too thin to make any accusations stick. He was too slick and clever a man to get caught. Well, almost.

When McMann got word of the killing of Dry-Hole Charlie, he considered the animosity that existed between the Dutch Henry and the Hicks organizations. Tensions had been growing taut for some time and the accusations of who had done what to whom, were flying in all directions. McMann more than suspected that Reynolds' hand was directly involved in the killing of Andrew McCracken, and felt the time was right to find out just how deep the conspiracy went.

There was a knock on his door and when Rex opened it, a man handed him a sealed envelope and disappeared. McMann gave Rex some orders and the man disappeared out of the hotel room and then out the back door into the night. It took him all of ten minutes to make his way through the side streets and back alleys to Fifth Street and then a few more minutes to get himself settled down in his hiding place in the back of a particular car. Once there he seemed to slow his heartbeat and relax. Rex had an uncanny way of catnapping anywhere he wished, but to add to his already unnerving image was that he seemed to sleep with his eyes open, and he would wake up at the sound of nothing, even before it could be heard.

When Rex was alerted by the sound of the uneven, staggering footsteps approaching the car, he made his extra large body disappear deep into the back seat. As the door opened and the intoxicated driver flopped into the seat, Rex controlled his breathing so as not to give himself away. The car started up and slowly made its way along the back roads out of town. After about 20 minutes, Reynolds heard an unfamiliar voice direct him to pull the car over. The presence of the cold steel of a pistol pressing against his neck persuaded him it was the right thing to do.

"I don't know who you are, mister, but I can tell you one thing, you're a dead man," Reynolds said, his speech both sneering and slurred. Nobody had ever threatened him and gotten away with it, not since Darwin drilled a hole in Louis' forehead with a slug from his derringer.

"What do you want, buster?" Reynolds demanded as he pulled the car to a stop. "I ain't got much money, but if it will get you off my back then here it is." As he turned, he expected to catch the would-be two-bit thief off guard. He held his wallet with his right hand and while reaching back with the wallet, he was bringing his left hand which held his gun around to shoot the would-be thief through the back seat.

Rex was expecting nothing less and was, in fact, a bit disappointed in how predictable Reynolds' move had been. He figured him for a wise-guy with better moves than that. Perhaps the liquor had clouded his senses. At any rate, before Reynolds could make his move, the butt of Rex's gun struck his head and laid him out cold.

As Reynolds later started to come to, it was with a splitting headache. He tried to focus his eyes, but then came to the realization that he could not see through the burlap sack which had been placed over his head. He also discovered that his hands were tied and that he seemed to be stretched face up, over the front end of his own car. After struggling a bit he gave up; the fatigue brought on by the blow to his head as well as the tremendous amount of alcohol he consumed made it pointless. He just relaxed his muscles and tried to figure out what had happened.

"You don't appear to be very comfortable there, Mr. Reynolds."

Reynolds jumped to the end of the restraints then yelled, "What the hell do you want, mister? You better let me go if you know what's good for you. Why, I'll kill ya, ya son-of-a-bitch!"

With that his head almost exploded from the pressure of yelling coupled with the alcohol and the knock on the head. Rex didn't reply for a while, he just stood by and let Reynolds worry a bit. He figured Reynolds had always been the one with the upper hand and wanted him to see what it felt like to be the victim for once.

When Rex didn't reply Reynolds stayed quiet for as long as he could, but finally after several minutes asked, "What do you want, mister?"

"Who ordered the hit on Andrew McCracken?" Rex inquired.

Reynolds convulsed in a spurt of energy pulling futilely at his ropes, and yelled, "What the hell are you asking me for, you bastard? You are messing with the wrong hombre, amigo. You better cut me loose and get the hell out of town while you have a chance."

Rex didn't respond.

After another few minutes Reynolds began, "Who the hell are you, and what makes you think I have any information to give you? Even if I knew anything at all, nothing in this world would make me tell you."

Rex didn't answer and after a few minutes pulled out his tinker's blade which he kept hidden on his body, somewhere out of sight and started honing the razor-sharp blade on a small whet stone he carried with him. Reynolds recognized the sound immediately and felt a cold chill run up his back. He started sweating and tried to calm his breathing. He was on the wrong end of this event. This was all bad.

Rex quietly walked over to where Reynolds lay and started inspecting Jacks right hand. He paused and inspected the spot where Jack's little finger once was, then asked Jack, "What happen here Mr. Reynolds, did your mother bite it off?" Reynolds kicked wildly with his feet and yelled all kinds of profanities. Rex allowed him to play himself out then approached Reynolds again inspecting his right hand.

Reynolds controlled his emotions anticipating what Rex would say next. He was smarter than this turd and would have to outsmart him.

When Rex grabbed the index finger of Reynolds right hand, Reynolds knew fear for maybe the first time. Rex didn't hesitate. He pinned the finger against the car fender and quickly chopped right through the bone. Reynolds screamed with pain as he was relieved of the second finger of his right hand. The pain was terrible, but hearing the crunching sound as the blade did its business, was too much for Reynolds. The last thing he remembered hearing as he lost consciousness were the words from the stranger's mouth. "Maybe next time you will have a better memory."

When Darwin found him the next morning, still tied to the hood of the car pulled off to the side of the road only a couple of miles from the house, Reynolds was close to dead. He had lost a lot of blood even though there was a string tied around the severed finger acting like a tourniquet. It seemed obvious to Darwin that whoever had cut off Jack's finger, had purposely slowed the blood flow just enough to keep him alive, but not enough to allow for a speedy recovery. No, Jack would be out of commission for several days, if he even lived.

The loss of Reynolds as the eyes and ears of the organization worried Darwin and he was hesitant to mention what had just happened to Hicks. Reynolds was the best "snake" in the Hicks organization. That he had, up to then, proven invincible was the main reason that Hicks had not employed another with even half his skills. This was a big blow. As Darwin drove the semiconscious Reynolds back to the Double Bar 7, he wondered what had gone wrong with their plan.

Hicks Falters

Hicks was visibly shaken to see what had happened to Reynolds. Maybe not so much for the pain and trauma bestowed on him, as much as the obvious insult and lack of respect the assailant showed in carrying out such an act. Reynolds was a wise and cunning man, he wasn't one to allow himself to be bushwhacked like this. He must be getting careless, he thought, or was feeling too comfortable. This was not the time for mistakes, too much was at stake.

Hicks considered the events of the last two days. After the court ruling where Lindsey had double-crossed him, he had stormed into town to have a word with him. That scrawny attorney of McCracken's offered to buy him out. What was that about? Hicks was not feeling well, his cough was getting worse, and with all this commotion he was getting tired. What else had happened? Leaving the courthouse, he'd headed over to the Riggins, a place he rarely visited. In fact, few people had really seen Hicks in several years. He'd even walked into the Riggins all alone, something he would

have never done before. When he left for the courthouse he didn't tell anyone, he just left.

And there was Dry-Hole Charlie. The gusher he'd hit
was one of the largest in the history of the United
States. It was blowing oil 20 feet in diameter and 200
feet in the air. This strike would have made Dry-Hole
Charlie a rich man. He undoubtedly held Hicks accountable for the loss of his fortune, and was apparently mad enough to want Hicks dead. Hicks realized
he had set himself up as a sitting duck. If Reynolds
hadn't caught up with him he may have ended up
dead.

Maybe, Hicks thought, he was getting too comfortable
as well. He decided to keep to the ranch and allow
Darwin to do most of the ground work.

As his mind went back to the events of the last few
days, he tried to figure out who could have done this to
Reynolds. Reynolds was as smart as they come and not
one to be caught off guard. Who could have called the
hit? Who wanted him dead? He had to laugh because
that was such a stupid question, no one in town cared
for Reynolds nor did they care if he lived.

When Hicks first met Jack he was about twelve years
old and even then was wound up like an angry sidewinder. He showed up on the back of that horse with
the fading remains of a black eye and bruises on most
of his body. Jack had said he was injured in the earthquake, but Hicks could see through his story. Those

bruises were administered by someone with a club. They were arranged in a pattern too symmetrical to be random.

This kid could take a lot and say nothing. Hicks considered the now second missing finger on Reynolds' right hand. This was the act of a skilled inquisitor. Someone had wanted information and when it was not forthcoming, he made his point. He left Jack with something to think about.

Hicks knew Jack would say nothing. He was someone who would never back up. There just wasn't any "give-in" in him. He would die, and enjoy dying, knowing his killer would end up with no answers, just a dead body.

But who was the butcher? He seemed more of a surgeon by the skill taken in the amputation. Dutch Henry was a hothead and could have called the hit on Reynolds himself. Dry-Hole Charlie had been working for him; was this a payback? What information could he have wanted from Reynolds?

Then there was that rat-faced little attorney, McMann. Hicks dismissed that idea with a shrug. That wimp couldn't have done it; he wouldn't have had the strength to do it. Then he remembered taking a swing at McMann in the courthouse; how did he miss that little prick? All he remembered was being helped up from the floor. That turncoat Judge Harry Lindsey was just sitting there with a smirk on his face. He'd deal with him later.

Hicks' reverie was interrupted as Darwin entered the library. "He's still unconscious, Unc. I've never seen him look so helpless. Whoever did this to him was trying to break his spirit. Judd went to town for the doc. He should be here soon. What made you go to that saloon by yourself, Unc? You trying to get yourself killed? We're too close now. Ain't no time to go and get yourself shot up."

Hicks walked over to a small side table and picking up a crystal decanter, poured himself a whisky. Darwin abstained.

"Whoever cut off Jack's finger must have kept it. I looked around for it but found nothing. The ground had been swept clean so there were no footprints or any other evidence I could find. There was no sign of another car, so the cutter must have been in the car with Jack. Jack either knew the man or he was hidden in back. Jack smelled of liquor, Unc. He'd been drinking more and more. I don't know what's gotten him so careless."

Hicks considered the information. Life had gotten complicated. He asked Darwin to follow him as he walked out of the library into the veranda garden. He had established a beautiful ranch here. Judd, older than dirt, still managed to run the place. He had over 3,000 head of beef, most of it young stuff. He remembered the first steers he and Judd drove in here some 35 years before. Not one of them legally his, every one of them wearing another ranch's brand.

Life seemed so much fun then. The Old West was still alive. The Hole in the Wall Gang was making so much trouble that smaller rustlers like himself were overlooked. Most of the crimes were blamed on Butch Cassidy's gang. He'd met Cassidy once. Liked him, he was kind of a gentleman in a way, but always thinking. Hicks would have joined his gang if he could, but he had been shot in the leg rustling cattle and couldn't ride just then. Butch told him to look him up when he healed up.

Hicks thought about that and about the news of Butch Cassidy and Sundance being shot to pieces down in Bolivia. No, he'd done the right thing. He was still alive and most of the old gang were buried deep or lay out in the desert with sun bleached bones picked clean of anything that was once them.

"I want you to go into town Dar, go tell that good for nothing sheriff what happened to Reynolds. Tell him I want answers. Tell him I pay him too well, and remind him that I know that he is a wanted man. There are people back east who would love to know his whereabouts. If he wants to keep his job and keep breathing, he better come up with some answers and fast. I want to know who attacked Reynolds. Tell him to investigate Dutch and that little prick attorney and anyone else he can think of. This thing stops here!"

Darwin heard his cue. Hicks would say no more. He expected Darwin to leave him to his thoughts.

The Back-up Plan

On his way into town, Darwin considered his options. He had been saving his money for years. Even the money he stole off of the dead man back in San Francisco still sat in his safe. He hadn't spent a penny of it. He rarely drank and Hicks gave him an expense account so almost every dollar he ever earned he stuck away. He'd skimmed quite a bit off of Hicks over the years as well. He figured he had about $300,000 in all. Some of it was in the bank in Monterey, but most of it he kept as cash hidden in the wall of his bedroom. No one knew about it, not even Jack.

Jack was a fool with money. He spent it as fast as he earned it. He had his favorites down on Fifth Street. He'd grab a bottle of tequila and spend the night drinking and screwing. There were two girls he favored and he would pick between; both were pretty and both were game. He'd come home early in the morning then sleep it off.

Darwin had known Jack most of his life and considered him as much family as he had. Uncle Ray was a cunning businessman and had taught him a lot, almost everything he knew, but his Uncle was becoming too careless. He was sick now and Darwin knew he was coughing up more and more blood. He never let on that he knew, he just observed.

Now 28 years old, the young man had his own plans. He wasn't sure how much longer Hicks was going to live, but he wasn't counting on his money anyway. In addition to the cash, he had secretly purchased 40 acres in the Kettleman Hills and expected to strike it rich once he could spud in. He had followed Andrew McCracken one afternoon several months back and watched as he explored around the site, poked around and seemed to find something interesting.

After McCracken left, Darwin went to see what he was looking at. Darwin knew nothing about geology, but he knew oil when he saw it. There was bubbling crude seeping right out of the ground. It formed a small pool before seeping back into the earth a few feet away. Yep, this was his ticket. He went to the department of land management office and purchased the parcel under a fictitious business name. He had done this for Hicks so many times the clerk didn't even think twice about it.

The fact was, Darwin also owned three other parcels in Coalinga's surrounding Kettlemen Hills, and also a small piece of land in Monterey. On a trip to the coast to check on the cannery's books for Hicks, he'd stayed a few extra days. He'd missed the tepid San Francisco climate he'd grown accustomed to as a boy; the desert was too hot and dry. The aesthetic coast of Monterey provided a radical change. The fog and ocean breeze settled his nerves. It was on that trip he found a small parcel. The old man who owned it had died and there were no heirs. Darwin put down $1,000 cash on the spot and the county clerk gave him a bill of sale.

Darwin pulled up in front of the sheriff's office and walked in. Murray was laid back in his chair, with his feet up on the desk, fast asleep. Darwin found it humorous, thinking this man was about as good as the law got in Coalinga. When he slammed the door, Murray awoke with a start. He bounced to his feet trying to focus on who the wake-up call was. When he saw Darwin standing there he was both annoyed and alarmed at the same time. Darwin never sought him out openly, usually sending word that he needed to meet with him at a prearranged place and time. That he had showed up in his office concerned him.

Murray sat back down in his chair and gestured to Darwin to find one for himself. "What gives, Anthony, what brings you to town?"

Darwin explained what happened to Reynolds. He told him about the set-up and the crime scene. Darwin knew Murray understood the implications. Reynolds was a smart man and would not be caught easily. The assailant was cunning and no doubt a professional. O'Malley's death was an execution and a warning, of that Murray had no doubt. O'Malley's body had been burned almost beyond recognition.

The fact that Reynolds was taken so easily was even more unnerving. Being Sheriff of Coalinga had been an easy job, at first. Murray had collected his paycheck from the county and his bribe money from Hicks. No one bothered him and most crimes were ignored unless Hicks wanted something done about them. But things were getting too hot now. Bigger things were at stake. Andrew McCracken's death had seemed such an easy thing, business as usual, really, but now all hell was breaking loose.

"Hicks wants this wrapped up quickly, Murray. He wants you to find out who is behind the attack on Reynolds and put it to bed."

"How the hell am I supposed to do that, Anthony? Why don't you go ask Reynolds who did it, if he ain't dead yet?"

"Listen, Murray," Darwin said. "Reynolds is still unconscious, he may not even make it through the day. I suggest you go put the pressure on the Dutch organization. You know that Dry-Hole Charlie tried to kill Hicks yesterday. Go investigate and find out what Dutch Henry knows. He sold that claim to McCracken's dad. There is something wrong there and maybe he is ready to talk. Or you can make him. No one wants to sell a gusher like that; he had to be strong-armed somehow."

A thought came to Darwin and he asked the sheriff, "What do you know about McMann? He's another story. He ramrodded that court hearing through as though he was judge and jury. He's too slick. I don't like him."

Darwin paused for a minute then continued. "Hicks is fit to be tied about losing that claim. I've never seen him like this, Murray. We better clean this up and get on with our plan before it's too late and we lose everything we've worked for."

The Box

When I got to *The Record* that morning, Mac was already there. He handed me a small box wrapped in butcher paper. There was a note on it addressed to me. Mac said that it was sitting on his desk when he arrived at work that morning. Nobody knew how it got there, it was just there when we opened up. I unfolded the note and read it, "Please deliver the contents of this box to Sheriff Murray. You should be present when he opens it." It was unsigned.

Curiosity got the best of us, so Mac and I decided to go visit the Sheriff right then. This was getting too interesting. When we walked into the office, Darwin and Murray were in a deep and heated conversation. Once they saw us they cut the conversation short. They both sat there like they'd eaten the canary.

I broke the silence with the comment, "Ran the story on Dry-Hole this morning, Murray. Seems the town wants answers. Word around town says Dry-Hole Charlie didn't own a gun."

Turning my gaze to Darwin I asked, "What brings you to town, Darwin? Don't seem to see you much these days."

"I come in to see the Sheriff about some personal business, which ain't none of yours," Darwin replied. The last few words had a sharper edge to them.

"Where's Reynolds, Darwin?" I asked. "People in Dutch's camp are on the verge of getting some answers themselves."

Turning my attention back to Murray, I stated, "If you don't pull Reynolds in for questioning, Sheriff, I'm thinking you may be run out of town on a rail, maybe even tarred and feathered."

Darwin looked at me through haunted eyes then addressed me directly. "Reynolds is out of it, McCoy. He was hit last night. He's up at the ranch hanging on for his life." Darwin went on to explain how he found Reynolds that morning strung out to dry on the hood of his own car. He told him about the deliberate brushing clean of the crime scene. Everyone remained silent for some time, each alone with their thoughts.

I broke the silence. "There's big money coming into town, boys. I think the jig here is up. Any of the small-town swindlers better pack it up and leave town while they got a chance." I was thinking how exciting this town was beginning to be. This town was ripe with stories, and as an investigative journalist, I was the man for the job.

Mac nudged me, reminding me of why we were there. I walked over to the Sheriff's desk and handed him the box. "Someone left this at *The Record*. Note on it says I'm to bring it over here and witness you opening it."

Murray looked at me then picked up the box suspiciously. He read the note then took out a knife and cut the string. Then he unwrapped the paper and opened the box. When he looked at the contents, he jumped and dropped the box on the desk. As he did so, a bloody finger rolled out on the desk. The room was as silent as a morgue. Nobody moved and nobody talked.

Finally Mac broke the silence saying, "Where the hell did that come from? And I wonder who's missing it?"

Looking around the room my eyes fell on the face of Darwin. He looked as though he had seen a ghost and was as white as the one he'd seen. "Do you know anything about this, Darwin?" I asked on impulse.

"That finger belongs to Jack. I found him this morning up on the Grade. Whoever ambushed him last night strapped him to the hood of his car and tied a burlap sack over his head. There was a string tourniquet tied around the stump of the index finger on his right hand."

Suddenly Darwin grabbed the string that was tied around the box, it was the same as was used on Reynolds and he said as much. "It was tight enough to slow the flow but not stop it. He ain't dead but he could as well be. When I found him this morning he was barely breathing."

We all stood silent for a few minutes, each considering what was about to take place. Reynolds had always been a force to be reckoned with. Up until this moment, there was no one person in town considered as dangerous or as cunning as Jack Reynolds. The fact that he had been taken so easily was shocking.

"Whoever could get the best of Reynolds is a dangerous man," Mac said to no one in particular. Each of us had our suspicions. There was something big about to happen in Coalinga and it wasn't looking pretty.

My own thoughts went to one person. Rex had the power and the ability to best Reynolds. It was doubtful if there was another person who could. I was pretty sure that no matter what the true facts were, Rex would have an alibi that was iron clad.

"I'm going to have to look into this," Murray said. "Reynolds is a solid citizen of Coalinga. Someone will pay for this." His words fell on muted ears, for there wasn't a one of us who believed Murray could get to the bottom of anything.

Back at the International

Mac and I left Darwin and Murray alone with their problems. We headed back to *The Record*, and as we were about to walk in the door, I told Mac I would be back soon. I made my way to the International. Mc-Mann was sitting at a table enjoying a nice lunch when I walked in. As I approached his table McMann addressed me. "Been expecting you, Mr. McCoy, won't you please have a seat?" He gestured to the empty chair across from him. It was no surprise to me that the place was set with hot coffee waiting. "What news do you have for me, Mr. McCoy? I hear that the nice young fellow, Dry-Hole Charlie, I think that is what they call him, was killed last night in a bar brawl. It seems so unfortunate after hitting such a rich strike."

I outlined the details of the event regarding Charlie, Hicks, and Reynolds being at the Riggins, even though I was sure I wasn't telling him anything he didn't already know.

Just then a waiter appeared, and McMann asked me to join him for a bite to eat. But I had no appetite, not after what I had seen on the sheriff's desk.

"Mr. McMann," I began, "It seemed Reynolds was bushwhacked last night and nearly killed." When McMann offered no comment, I continued. "Thing is, Mr. McMann, I thought you might have some information for me. It seems that someone relieved Reynolds of another of his fingers."

"Interesting," McMann said and then paused. "They must be valuable commodities. Between oil and Reynolds' fingers, Coalinga seems the land of opportunity! So where is Two-Finger Jack now?" I hadn't seen much emotion in McMann other than the momentary tenderness for the dead dog and during the meeting with Lou. Now I saw a bit of a sense of black humor in his eyes. And he was confirming to me that he knew the details of what had happened to Reynolds. Was this the first slip-up McMann had made? Was he beginning to get too comfortable with me?

"I believe he is barely hanging onto his life up at the Double Bar 7. He may not make it. When Darwin found him, he had almost bled out and was barely breathing."

McMann was taking a sip of his tea. He paused and then asked. "Who do you think could have done such a thing?"

I hesitated a minute then commented. "I haven't noticed Rex lurking behind any curtains this morning, is he not well?" McMann while inspecting his well-manicured fingernails stated, "Rex is on a train to Chicago as we speak. He left yesterday morning. I sent him to care for Lou's sister Sadie. Seems she needed some assistance in her move to New Mexico."

That Rex would have been recognized boarding the train was not a question. McMann was too smart not to make sure that there were plenty of witnesses to verify Rex's alibi. My assumption was he got off the train unseen at the next stop and was picked up by one of McMann's unseen army of eyes which he had alluded to. He would have then hid in the shadows awaiting the opportunity to shanghai the over-confident Reynolds.

I had no doubt that Rex would have tried to extract information from Reynolds. Knowing what I did about Jack, I was pretty certain that Rex would walk away none the wiser. Reynolds was a man who would never break. He would die with sealed lips.

Testing my theory I asked, "Mr. McMann, tell me, has Rex dug up any new information regarding who killed Andrew McCracken?"

McMann looked at me through slightly humored eyes and replied, "So far, it seems that anyone who may be in the know is either afraid to come forward, is dead, or too tight-lipped. I have no doubt that something will break soon though."

Arriving back at *The Record* I found a note on my desk scribed in the fine hand I knew to be that of Lou Williams. It was sealed with the wax stamp she used which bore the impression of a Scottish castle on it. Sitting down I broke the seal and opened the letter. It was brief, "Meet me at the shack, 12 midnight tonight. Bring Mr. McMann." That was it. What was Lou up to? What information had she come up with?

I decided I should get word to McMann right away, since he seemed to have a way of disappearing. Not finding him in the restaurant I ascended the stairway leading to his room. I reached the top of the stairs just in time to see a man duck out of McMann's room and out of a hall window above the back alley. I found McMann rising up from the floor somewhat shaken. A cut over his right eye was liberally oozing blood down his face and onto his white shirt.

"He got the best of me, McCoy," McMann said. "He must of heard me coming down the hall and cold cocked me as soon as I walked in the door."

"Did you get a look at him?" I asked.

"No," he said. "It happened too quickly."

As I looked around the room I could see the intruder had rifled through everything, all McMann's clean white shirts were tossed on the floor as were his matching suits. The desk and dresser drawers were all out and piled on the floor. Whoever did this must have known McMann's daily routines; they'd had time to do a thorough search.

McMann was standing at the sink in his bathroom dabbing his wound with a damp cloth and inspecting the damage to his head in the mirror. There was a cut just below the hairline above his right eye. It was about two inches long.

"Looks like you might need some stitches, Mr. McMann."

He looked at me through the reflection in the mirror and replied without addressing my remark, "What are you doing here McCoy? What do you want?" His demeanor resembled that of a python, his gaze was piercing and seemed to take in every fiber of my existence. He was a man who was always perfect in his presentation, to see him so out of sorts was a bit unnerving.

Olive-Green Fibers

I told him of the note from Lou. This seemed to snap him out of his frame of mind, and suddenly again he was Mr. McMann. He asked me to wait for him in the lobby, that he would be down in ten minutes. Understanding his desire to put himself in order I turned to leave him to his wound and torn up room. As I was about to walk out the door, I noticed a few strands of olive-green fiber hanging on the strike plate of the door latch. The assailant must have caught some garment on it as he raced out the door. I glanced in McMann's direction, and as he was preoccupied tending to his wound, I dislodged a strand and placed it in the small notebook I always carried. I was certain McMann's investigation of the room would come up with the remaining evidence, and was more than curious to observe where the trail would lead. One thing I knew for sure though, whoever it was that clobbered McMann on the head was a dead man.

As I descended the stairs back down to the lobby, my thoughts focused on the whereabouts of Rex the Terrible. I also recalled McMann mentioning his "eyes on the ground." Where were these men now, and how come they weren't protecting McMann? I guessed he must have had them spread out snooping around town.

Things were happening pretty fast around here, even for Coalinga. There were a few big players in town but that didn't discourage the many ambitious wildcatters from grappling for position. Money was money, but it took talent, understanding of geological formations, and more than a bit of luck to strike it rich in the oil business. Dry-Hole Charlie was dead, but there were others in his camp who stood to lose a fortune with the sale and acquisition of his recent strike. Dutch Henry's decision to sell it so quickly was a curious thing. Why would he sell what could be the biggest strike in history so readily? I began to become suspicious of that transaction and wondered about any prior affiliation there might have been between the McCracken empire and Dutch Henry's company.

I was sitting in the hotel lobby sipping coffee awaiting McMann's arrival when Rex walked in the front door of the hotel, apparently returning from a quick trip to New Mexico. He took me in without so much as a smile then proceeded up the stairs to McMann's room. Again, I was impressed with the grace with which such a big man could carry himself. He seemed to glide across the floor, his feet barely touching it as he went. I began to wonder about his character and who he really was.

Somehow, he reminded of a man I once met or perhaps had read about, and I wanted to figure this out. Perhaps this could help me uncover the secret details I needed to blow this whole affair wide open. I did enjoy the intrigue, and as a journalist, drank in the suspense. But another factor was that the patience of the citizens of Coalinga was wearing dangerously thin; and people were scared. It seemed the whole town was about to explode, like one of the geysers which defined its very existence.

I looked up to see McMann descending the stairs. He appeared as he always did, well-manicured, brushed up, and immaculate. There was a tidy piece of tape covering the newly acquired lesion, which seemed to go unnoticed by the uninvolved. Rex was nowhere to be seen, and I was sure he was off looking for a victim clad in an olive-green suit who would most likely soon be tucked into a shallow desert grave. No doubt his broken body would show the volume of the interrogation involved in his untimely demise.

McMann seated himself across from me, then beckoning the waiter, ordered whiskey, one for each of us. I'd never seen him drink before and realized his facade did well to cover up what must have been a shock to his pride. McMann was not one to be caught off guard. The fact that he had allowed himself to be blind-sided, in his own room, was probably more than he could fathom. It would not go unavenged. I could only pity, to some degree, his assailant.

McMann sipped his whiskey and said nothing. I chose to do the same, appreciating the suspense and enjoying the moment. McMann snapped his fingers alerting the waiter again and beckoned for the bottle. The waiter obliged and left quickly, understandably unnerved by the little man's demeanor. McMann poured himself another shot and me the same. We sat in silence for what seemed an eternity, until finally McMann spoke. "Who do you suppose wears an olive-green coat, Mr. McCoy?"

The question rocked me at first, but what made me think McMann would miss two things in the same minute? "Rex has the remaining threads and I expect will no doubt answer that question for us in the next hour." McMann declared, "I'll have those threads in your notebook, Mr. McCoy. You see I'm a careful man and can have no loose ends about."

Reflecting on my knowledge of McMann I felt the fool for assuming that I could put anything over on him. I opened my notebook and placed the fibers on the white tablecloth in front of McMann. He removed a white silk handkerchief from his pocket then delicately retrieved the evidence. He folded it neatly, then placed it in another pocket. That I was to say nothing of this incident was not a question, and I thought McMann had come to know me well enough to know that I understood this to be the case. I actually felt a bit of pride in that I had this respect from him, strange as it seemed.

"Now, what of Miss Williams?" McMann asked. I took the note out of my pocket and placed it in front of him. After reading it, he folded it neatly and placed it in his pocket.

The Twelve-O-Three

"I will ask a favor of you, Mr. McCoy. Dutch Henry has some papers for me. They need to be taken to the train station this morning. I would have had Rex take them, but he seems to have an urgent assignment and will not be available. There is a man named Bean who will be arriving on the twelve-o-three. I would appreciate it if you would pick them up from Mr. Henry's office and deliver them to Bean along with this." McMann pulled an envelope out of his inside coat pocket and placed it on the table in front of me. The envelope was addressed to one "Sadie Arnold, Santa Fe, New Mexico". It appeared to contain a large amount of cash. "Sadie is in the care of Dr. Johnson now. He is Mr. McCracken's personal physician. She requires quite a bit of care on an immediate basis. Mr. McCracken insisted that we start her treatment right away even though Miss Williams has not yet fulfilled her obligation. Mr. McCracken is a compassionate man, Mr. McCoy, he also appreciates those people who appreciate him." With that McMann excused himself from the table. As he turned he remarked, "I will see you at midnight, Mr. McCoy." Then he turned and walked away.

I'm not sure how long I remained at the table. The events of the day were rolling through my head. It seemed that enough had happened this morning to fill a week's worth of papers, and the tempo was not seeming to slow.

Presently, Mac walked into the International and found me at the table with my mind elsewhere. I looked up to see him staring at the half empty bottle of whiskey with a worried look on his face. Mac was a teetotaler and was obviously a bit startled to see the bottle in front of me, especially since it was not yet noon.

"Are you all right, Alex?" he asked. "Maybe you need some time up at the lake."

I shook myself out of my thoughts and snapped back to the reality of the moment. Looking up at Mac I chuckled and said, "It's been quite a morning Mac. Don't worry about the bottle; it belonged to McMann. Although I must admit, I was compelled to join him for a shot or two."

Mac laughed and said "I can't say as I blame you. If I were a drinking man I'd probably join you. It's not often your morning starts with a gift of a severed finger, gift-wrapped at that."

I saw Mac's gaze go to the envelope that sat in front of me. Following his gaze, I picked it up and stuck it away in my pocket.

"Should I ask?" Mac inquired.

"Not at the moment," I replied. "I will fill you in once I have something to report."

I again noted to myself how very lucky I felt that I was on the right side of this equation.

Suddenly I remembered the favor McMann asked of me and almost knocked the table over as I jumped to my feet. Mac looked at me as though I'd been stung by a fire ant, but before he could say anything I said, "Sorry, Mac, I have a train to catch," and I hurried out the door.

My dilemma was finding Dutch Henry at his office and making it over the grade in time to meet the twelve-o-three before she left for Bakersfield.

When I entered Henry's office he was leaning back in his chair with his boots crossed on his desk. There was the thick smell of a fine cigar, and he had *The Record* open and was reading my column on the latest land grab. That, of course, being the court case involving Dutch, Dry-Hole Charlie, and Raymond Hicks. He lowered the paper as I entered to see who was disturbing his privacy. I was more than surprised to see a big smile across his face. This did not seem the face of a man who was just swindled out of one of the biggest oil strikes in United States history.

There was obviously more to this story than I was yet privy to, and I was determined to live long enough to see it through. But with that in mind, I reminded myself to box up my latest journals and send them off to Ma, who would put them in the barn for safe keeping. One never knew what could happen and when. People seemed to have their lives cut short a bit too often in Coalinga these days.

"Morning Dutch," I began, "you seem mighty happy today."

He lowered his feet from the desk and stood up to greet me. "Morning Alex." As he rounded the desk to shake my hand I marveled at the strength of the man. His powerful build reminded me of a smaller version of Rex, thick as an oak tree with skin so weathered it resembled an old wrangler's worn out saddle. His hands were as big as my head, as hard as anvils and had the grip of a vise.

"What brings you around here, son?" Dutch was in his early 50s but he was well-weathered. I didn't take the greeting as condescending.

"Seems I'm an errand boy for George McMann today. Apparently I'm to deliver some papers to a Mr. Bean down at the station. He will be expecting me before the whistle blows for the twelve-o-three."

"Of course, of course, Alex, got 'em right here." Dutch moved over to the rather large Wells Fargo bank safe that sat in the corner of his office and keeping his back to me, scrolled through the numbers and then spun the big wheel. There was a big clank as the bolts retracted and an ominous squeak as he swung the door open. It disturbed the stillness of the room as if the door opening sucked in the air.

I got a gander at some of the contents in the safe as Dutch pulled a folder from a pile of documents. I could see stacks of money off to one side, enough to please a prince. There were several scrolls standing on end, which would document each and every claim in the Henry oil fields, whether active, dead, or yet unexplored. I noticed his 1911 Colt .45 hanging in a holster on the inside of the door, as well as the double barreled sawed-off 12-gauge, better known as a coach gun, leaning in the corner of the safe. Dutch no doubt was ready for any foul play regarding his office belongings. He also was a big game hunter and loved his weapons. As he swung the door closed, spun the wheel to the safe, and returned to his desk, I was admiring some of the contents of his rather large office.

Lining one wall was a rack containing several Henry repeating rifles, enough to arm a regiment. Dutch's grandfather, I knew, was Benjamin Tyler Henry, the namesake and designer of the famed Henry repeating rifle. This was an amazing weapon and went into production around 1866. It was a famous rifle of the old west, yet first became popular with the Union Army during the Civil War. There were about 8,000 manufactured in all and their ability to carry 16 loads was a huge advantage over the muzzle-loader armed Reb soldiers of the South. Later, several of these rifles found their way west, notably in the hands of the Sioux and Cheyenne Indians after their obliteration of General George Armstrong Custer and his doomed U.S. 7th Cavalry unit at the Little Bighorn in Montana in 1876. Anyway, the rifles were beautifully kept and a pride to Dutch's collection.

I was also amazed at the collection of fossils Dutch had hanging on the walls and set out on a long table stacked against the far wall. There were large rocks split in half that revealed strange fish-like creatures from another world or time; ancient skulls and jaw bones of extinct animals including one of his greatest prizes, that of a saber-toothed tiger. But what was of greatest interest to me was a 20-foot long mastodon tusk his crew had delivered to him last month. That it was petrified was a testimony to the ancient habitation of this now-dry desert. If the amount of oil below the surface was an indicator of the breadth of the vast prehistoric swampland which lay below the Coalinga desert floor, then it was hard to fathom.

"Here are the documents McMann needs." Dutch's voice broke through my distraction and reminded me of why I was here. "There's more where that came from, Alex," Dutch said as he noticed me taking a last look at the ominous tusk. "Come back when you have more time, I'd love to show you the rest of my collection."

The sincerity in Dutch's voice was refreshing. It seemed that most wildcatters and roughnecks were only interested in raping the land of its black gold, then heading for higher ground. Dutch seemed to have a genuine love for the land and of its history, more than anyone I'd met to date. Except for Andrew McCracken. Dutch told me that Andrew had invited some paleontologists out from the University of California at Berkeley to make a study of his collection next month, and he was looking forward to them shedding some light on some of his finds. He told me that I would be welcome to attend the meeting and that I might like to run an article on his finds. I told him that I would be honored.

Realizing time was short, I said my goodbye and rushed out the door to my rig. The twelve-o-three had a 30-minute stop for water delivery as well as supply drop off.

Coalinga's water was basically undrinkable so water was delivered weekly and piped into town. In fact, Coalinga was the only town in America that needed three taps in each kitchen sink. Two for hot and cold water respectively, and then one for drinking and cooking water. The water was really that bad.

As I pulled over the rise that led from the town to the depot, I saw the Southern Pacific Engine No. 25 pulling into the station. I was just pulling up as she slid to a stop. I decided to wait in the car and see who materialized. I didn't believe McMann would put me in harm's way deliberately, but my years as an investigative reporter had taught me to err on the side of caution. I reached for my Colt hanging from the steering column and felt the reassurance of its cold steel in my hand. I don't know why I did it, but I pulled it from its holster, checked its loads and then slipped it into my belt as I exited the car.

I found a corner of the station where there was only desert at my back and leaned against a post awaiting my clandestine rendezvous. As I watched the crew jump from the train and go to work preparing her for its next stop, I thought back on my pa and how he would leave so early in the morning to meet the old Number 3. How our horse, Old Pete, would drive Pa in our wagon to and fro every day. I thought about that fateful night when Pa was shot, the event that would ultimately shorten his days on earth. I felt that familiar tightening in the pit of my stomach as I remembered seeing him lying in bed, Ma caring for him night and day, pumping life back into him. I remembered when Old Pete found his way home the next morning, more the worse for wear, and minus the wagon. I thought about what Lou had told me about Hicks' secret visit to her shanty that very night. How she patched him up, wiping off the residual oil and keeping his secret all these years.

A man stepped from the train, who could only be Mr. Bean. That he resembled McMann didn't surprise me. These types of men had a certain way about them and the phrase "you can't judge a book by its cover" was appropriate since while they were dressed immaculately, they had the venom of a sidewinder.

Not looking at me, but assuming the person awaiting his arrival would catch the signal, he removed his dark brown velvet derby, inspected the feather for neatness, brushed off some imaginary dust, replaced it on his head then proceeded to the room which once was the old telegraph station. He hesitated before entering, brushing off his coat, but taking the time to casually locate any followers.

I decided to wait and observe a few minutes. I produced a cigarette from a holder I kept in my pocket. I didn't really smoke, but found cigarettes often useful to get others to feel comfortable around me, so that they might give forth more information than they first thought they should. I tried not to choke on the smoke and played the part of a lazy traveler who was stretching my legs before the next stretch of rails.

As I finished the smoke, I pulled a copy of *The Record* out of my back pocket and meandered over to the bench in front of the telegraph office. As I sat down and opened the paper pretending to read my own column, I was filled with a haunting emotion as I reflected on how many times I had visited my pa as he sat in that very office sending and receiving information which was transmitted along the lines.

I could hear the nervous pacing of the man in the derby hat as he awaited his appointment. After a couple of minutes I felt it safe to enter the office. Just as I entered the room, a man dropped down from the rafters knocking Mr. Bean on the head as he did. Bean went down hard and was clearly out of it. I must have surprised the assailant, for when he saw me, he jumped to his feet fumbling for something in his pocket all the while. Everything happened so fast I can only imagine what happened rather than recall it. As best as I can tell, the man pulled a pistol from his pocket and took a pot shot at me. Luckily, Bean had come to and kicked the man in his leg throwing off his point-blank aim. My reflexes took over at that point. Pulling my colt from my belt I let a round fly hitting the man in his right shoulder. The impact knocked the pistol out of his hand and knocked him back into the wall. He had a wild look in his eye and took a flying leap through back window, shattering the glass as he made his escape.

Bean was just getting up from the floor taking inventory of himself and his attire. I was anticipating that the gunshots would warrant the arrival of a railroad detective at any moment, and wanted to take care of business so I could hit the road as soon as possible. The railroad authorities still exercised their own jurisdiction, and would often act as judge, jury, and executioner all at the same time. They were never fun to deal with, and I wanted none of them. When they didn't arrive, I decided that the train whistle must have been blowing at the exact moment of the attack thus drowning out the blasts.

As Mr. Bean finished positioning his hat on his head, he looked at me with an inquisitive eye. "I believe I may owe my life to you, young man. I am forever in your debt." The last thing I wanted at that moment was a lifetime affiliation with this man and expressed as much. "If you are Bean, then I have some documents for you. Please identify yourself so we can get this business over with."

"I am Claude Bean. You are George McMann's courier then?"

The disdain with which those words hit me must have shown clearly on my face. "I am my own man Mr. Bean, and I am only here to help a friend in need." I produced both the documents Dutch had given me as well as the envelope addressed to Sadie Arnold. "I thank you for delivering this to Miss Arnold. Please tell her that her sister sends her regards."

Bean handed me a sealed letter addressed to George McMann. It was on the stationary of Angus McCracken. "Please deliver this to George for me." Bean said nothing more, merely turned toward the door, and without a gesture of goodbye disappeared though it. I thought it best to wait until the train pulled out of the station, hoping that our wounded attacker would be hidden away in some dark corner of an empty boxcar instead of waiting behind the station to take revenge on me.

Then I noticed his derringer lying on the floor and decided it would make a good souvenir, so I retrieved it. Opening it I noticed that both rounds were spent. When I looked behind me, I could see where two slugs had entered the wall. They were no more than 4 inches apart. Had it not been for the timely kick by Bean I would have been a dead man. Whoever it was had pulled both triggers at the same time. Whether by mistake or on purpose, had I been hit, it would have been a deadly proposition.

The Jumper

I arrived back at *The Record* office and went to find Mac at his desk. Before I could sit down he told me I needed to head over to Church Street. He'd just got a call regarding a jumper. Apparently, some roughneck had gotten all liquored up and in the midst of some depression, threw himself off of the clock tower.

I felt the winkles around my tired eyes deepen as I turned toward the door.

"Alex," Mac's voice stopped me, "Are you all right?"

Pausing I walked over to his desk and removing the derringer from my coat pocket placed it on his desk. "I will fill you in on how I procured this when I return." With that I walked out the door and worked my way up to Church Street.

Mac picked up the derringer and admired its pearl handle. It appeared to be an early model Remington .41 caliber. It had seen plenty of use, but was well kept. Mac removed the spent rounds, opened his desk drawer and placed it carefully on a silk handkerchief he kept there for emergencies. He was more than curious to get the lowdown on its procurement.

I was still a bit shaky from the encounter at the station, this feeling only became worse as I rounded the corner to Church Street. Sheriff Murray was there as was a growing crowd of citizens. As I approached, the broken and twisted body of the jumper came into view. Pushing my way through the crowd, I took in a scene which needed very little explanation. There, lying on the ground, was a would-be stranger. I say would-be, because the olive-green coat he was wearing filled in the blanks. What was more, his right-side pocket was facing up, and it was evident by the torn pocket where the door latch had caught as he made his escape. I assumed Rex had acquired the information he needed, or this man would still be alive, bound and gagged in some dark corner of a woodshed.

I was about to leave feeling a bit sick to my stomach, but just as I turned to go, Murray decided to move the body. The gasp from the crowd brought me back to determine their surprise. Whether a warning or just a signature I couldn't be sure, but the man's left ring finger was missing, and the bloody stump that remained was evidence that it had been attached that morning.

Rather than head back to *The Record* I walked over to the International, and as I expected, McMann was sipping tea, enjoying a light lunch. He looked up as I approached the table. "Ah, just in time for lunch. Won't you join me, Mr. McCoy?" I shouldn't have been amazed by his coolness but yet marveled at the man's nerve.

I didn't answer, and just stood there a bit in a daze.

McMann sipped his tea and then inquired. "All went well at the station then? Did Mr. Bean have any correspondence for me?"

Remembering the letter in my pocket, I extracted it and threw it on the table. "There was a jumper around the corner, McMann. It appears that some poor soul lost his wits and jumped from the bell tower. It's a shame he soiled his olive-green jacket." Searching for a reaction I found none.

Shortly McMann commented, "I'm not surprised, this desert is very depressing. In fact, the longer I stay the more anxious I become and the more I hate it. I look forward to returning to the east coast and the pleasant, cultured civilization it provides."

As I turned to leave, McMann reminded me, "Until midnight, Mr. McCoy. Oh, and you won't be followed."

McMann was beginning to get on my nerves. I felt like I had oil on my hands and no way to wash it off. He stuck to me like pine pitch.

Splintered Out of Reverie

I got up out of my over-stuffed chair feeling a bit re-
freshed. I had also found it necessary to take a long hot
bath and soak as much of the day's events out of me as
I could. I was only 40 years old, but these last several
days left me feeling like I was approaching 80. Walking
over to the kitchen to make myself a peanut butter
sandwich, I thought about my wife and kids. I was
relieved that they were away at the lake, safe from the
turmoil of the Coalinga oil grab.

I chuckled as I thought about the Orton clan and how
the three brothers were constantly one upping each
other. Bert was the youngest, and always the rabble
rouser. One afternoon we were all relaxing at the lake
while Virgil was taking a catnap while lying in a hammock tied between two trees. There was a particular
hatch of bugs that day that seemed to be attracted to
Virgil's particular smell or something and he had been
complaining about them to no end.

As he lay there snoring away in the cool of the afternoon sun, Bert sat close by whittling a whistle out of a

piece of pine. He couldn't help but notice Virgil's swatting away at the bugs as they swarmed around his head looking for some safe haven on which to light. He would slap at the bugs amid a chorus of snores, which would rival a concert of the Great Caruso, at least in volume.

Bert, in his never diminishing desire to aggravate his brother Virgil, slipped over to the cooking area and found a bottle of bitters. He stealthily crept up to where Virgil lay sleeping and skillfully dribbled a single drop of the bitters into Virgil's mouth. Then he replaced the bitters and returned to his whittling stump.

Presently Virgil began to stir, smacking his lips. Suddenly his eyes popped open wide and he scrambled to get up, causing the hammock to rollover. Virgil lay sprawling on the ground in a daze before he jumped to his feet smacking and spitting.

When Virgil related the terrible taste he woke up to, Bert said that he'd heard that those bugs that had been favoring him all day were full of poison, and if one got in your mouth, the bitter taste could slowly drive you mad. Virgil took off running like a shot, jumping wildly into the lake, splashing water into his mouth. When he finally returned to camp, he was met with an explosion of laughter as his other brother, Norman, recounted what had happened, once again implicating his younger brother Bert. Of course, Bert was nowhere to be found, thinking this a good time to hightail it up to Dinky Creek for some trout fishing. He knew that Virgil's temper would dampen by the time he returned, especially if he returned with a creel full of speckled Brookies.

I was recalling the terrified look on Virgil's face while mindlessly applying peanut butter to my bread when I was startled out of my revere with the untimely and loud ring of the telephone. I jumped, startled, moving to my left to grab for it. That phone call saved my life.

The cabinet door, which I had been standing in front of just moments before, suddenly exploded into splinters from the impact of a large caliber bullet. This was followed by the loud report of a high-powered rifle outside the window. Terrified, I hit the ground then lay frozen in place. Outside I heard the screeching tires of the getaway car as it zoomed away up the block and into the night.

Having lost my appetite, I crawled on my hands and knees to where the earpiece of the phone was swinging, hanging from the wall. Feeling it was now safe enough, I slowly stood putting the piece to my ear. I heard the familiar voice of Lou Williams.

"Alex, are you there? Alex, this is Lou." I could hear a concern in her voice as I drummed up enough voice to answer. "Yes, Lou, it's me. I'm okay."

"Thank God," she replied. "I called to warn you, but was afraid I might have been too late."

"If you hadn't called when you did Lou, it would have been. I would have been blown to smithereens. Whoever took a shot at me was using some kind of canon. It would have taken my head clean off."

"Alex, I'm afraid someone broke into my flat and tore the place apart. Everything I own has been rifled through. The whole the place is upside down."

"Where are you now, Lou. Are you safe?"

"I think so. I made my way to Peg's flat and she has me hidden here. I need to move though, I don't want to put her in danger."

"Okay," I said. "Can you get to the meeting place?" Knowing that someone could be listening at the county switchboard end of the line, I did not want to give the location away."

"Yes, I think so."

"Okay, get there as quickly as you can and keep out of sight."

I moved to the pantry and lifted a box of .38s off the shelf. I didn't know where this was going to lead, but I wasn't going in empty-handed. As I made my way out of the pantry I spotted a bottle of whisky beckoning to my thirst. Thinking better of it I let it lie, wanting nothing to deaden my response time. Things were happening fast before, and now they were speeding up even more. I needed all of my wits to stay alive. I found a dark hat and overcoat, and after turning off all the lights, I slipped out of the back door. Rather than move too quickly, I moved to the left and stood there motionless in the dark, not convinced that I was alone. The night seemed too quiet and still.

Goodbye to a Friend

Darwin sat motionless in the silent room. As he clutched the lifeless hand of the only friend he'd ever had, he reflected on the past many years. Alone together, the broken and spent souls emerged from the fires and broken ruins of what was once early century San Francisco. That freckle-faced, red-haired, iron-spirited little boy had grown into the backbone of the Hicks organization. Darwin hadn't considered it before, but together he and Reynolds had forged a union second to none.

They had risen out of the dust to the upper echelon of power that was Coaling Station A. True they had grown apart in the past many years and Darwin felt a bit of sorrow that he had not really taken the time to talk with Reynolds of late. Reynolds had gone to drinking more and more, he spent more time in the beds along Fifth Street than he did his own. Darwin had never really worried about Reynolds much. Even though they seldom talked, there was an unspoken understanding between them. At least Darwin thought there was. Darwin thought back to the day of the '06 quake, when he found Reynolds sitting behind a bush. Bloody and beaten – at least his body, but not his spirit. He remembered putting out a hand to the boy and bringing him under his fold. It wasn't a conscious thought; he just did it.

Darwin had known no love in his life. Whether his father had died a hero or coward, he'd never know. His mother would bed any man who came along. When the quake hit, he found freedom for the first time in his life. He had been his own man from that day on. He recalled riding though the Peachtree Valley and into the Double Bar 7, Raymond Hicks' ranch, he and Reynolds sitting atop of Old Willy. Vagabonds, yet clinging to some deeply buried idea that life was more than it seemed. He had done well. Both he and Reynolds had made a name for themselves. He as the heir apparent to the vast holdings of Raymond Hicks, and Jack Reynolds as the strong-armed enforcer. A man Darwin could count on, a man with no back-up of his own.

Yet here lay Jack, at least what was left of Jack. Just moments ago, Darwin held his hand desperately trying to pump life back into him. Reynolds had never regained consciousness, never opened his eyes. Darwin sat there helplessly as Jack took his last breath.

Then something hit Darwin, something he had never felt anything like before, and it was more than he could handle. A deep anguish overcame him and he began to sob, large tears rolling down his cheeks as he tried to control this strange emotion he knew not what it was. His body took over and convulsed with grief as he leaned over to embrace his lost friend.

The Old Hole in the Wall

Hicks had been sitting in his study, looking at all his books, again wondering why he'd never taken the time to read even one of them. His cough had worsened to a point where blood seemed to be more plentiful than saliva. He had a bottle of whiskey in front of him and had consumed more than half of it. His head was spinning with thoughts and emotions. Something seemed to have gone wrong, just when he was about to win the whole game.

The liquor seemed to have clogged his brain because it kept jumping from thought to thought. He was usually able to think things through quite clearly and to the end. That was a talent he'd always had. He'd know'd it, even old Butch had know'd it. That's why Butch had wanted him to join in as part of the gang back then. Butch was a good thinker and talker, while Sundance was a bit more wild-mannered and unpredictable. Butch had said Hicks could come along and help sit on Sundance now and then. Maybe together they could hold Sundance down and stop him from overreacting and getting everybody killed.

Those were the days, Hicks thought. Not a care in the world and anything and everything was yours for the grabbing. He'd been to the Hole in the Wall on several occasions. He'd rode with the likes of Laughing Sam Carey and Black Jack Ketchum on various stagecoach hold ups or bank robberies. He remembered the use of that now famous phrase, "Throw down the box," which echoed through the annals of time as the stagecoaches made their way across the wild and woolly west. Those days were gone now, and he thought about how he and old Judd plumb split out one day. Judd with his bad leg and all, but they left anyway and rode on out to California. They'd rustled plenty of cattle along the way, and probably rode into Priest Valley with more than a thousand head in all. Hicks chuckled and poured himself another drink. He was recalling riding through that herd. He must have counted over 30 different brands on them cattle, and not one of them his.

Now his thoughts turned to the present. Things were not good. Reynolds was dead. Dutch somehow had swindled him out of his oil. But Dutch seemed too happy to have lost that strike. So what was his affiliation with Old Man McCracken? What had Lindsey agreed to? Who was paying off Murray and what was the attorney, Bates, up to? All these things were swimming in whiskey as he decided on his next move.

He threw back the last of the whisky and slammed the empty bottle down on the table. "I'll be damned if I take this lying down. No greenhorn carpetbagger is going to swindle me out of what's rightfully mine. I'm going down to town and have a talk with that no-good Dutch Henry. I'll see what he has to say when he looks down the barrel of my .44 Winchester '73. I'd like to put a hole right through his heart. In fact, after I'm done getting the information I want, I might just do that."

Hicks stumbled to the rack of rifles racked along the wall of his study and chose the very gun he'd carried on all those Hole in the Wall raids. He pulled back the lever and slammed it shut. It was a natural reflex, nothing to it. Pulling a box of shells off of the shelf, he fed them into the rifle feeling the power of his youth, again loaded for bear.

Somehow he felt ageless. He was pushing 60 now but suddenly felt like one of the gang, racing for the safe confines of the Hole in the Wall after some midnight raid.

He felt good. Heading out to the barn, he found his Model A sitting in the corner, covered with a tarp. He ripped off the tarp, put his rifle on the seat and went to the front to crank 'er over. First try. She sputtered and choked but came to life much like his old horse would come to life once he smelled the blood of a raid. A good rustling horse loved the game. As he got into the seat and headed out the drive and up to the grade, he remembered his old horse, Buck. He was a strawberry roan, had one black sock and a black mane. Best horse he ever owned. Got shot out from under him though. Apaches got him outside of Mesa Verde. If it wasn't for Judd, some Apache would be riding bareback, carrying a lance with Hicks' scalp on it. Yep, Judd was one to ride the river with. Tough as they come. Never did figure him for no outlaw though. He'd lost his family coming west. Cheyennes killed 'em all, except for Judd. He hid out in the brush and watched all the while as the Cheyenne slaughtered his kin.

Judd was like an older brother to him, one he'd never had himself. Maybe that's why he took in Darwin and Reynolds. His mind kept racing as he made his way down the grade toward town.

The Encounter

After about an hour, he neared the building that housed Dutch Henry's office. As Hicks pulled to a stop a couple hundred yards out, he could see the midnight oil burning. Dutch was there as Hicks had hoped. He wanted to put an end to all this stuff and get back on track. Dutch had been a thorn in his side for far too long.

Dutch was sitting at his desk, studying the papers Andrew McCracken had given him. They all but spelled out the best drilling spots in the county. Henry had grown up back east. Fact was, his pa and old man McCracken were kin of some kind. No one knew it out west of the Mississippi, but Dutch Henry had been bankrolled by McCracken from the start. Angus McCracken had a large cotton plantation and also owned quite a bit of sugar cane off the coast on Jamaica. When McCracken's sister, Henry's aunt, introduced Angus and Dutch, Angus thought Dutch would be a good mentor to his young son, Andrew. Angus married late and was already 60 when Andrew was born. He was mid-80s now, still "strong as an ox and twice as stubborn," as his wife would say. Dutch was 30 years older than Andrew, but they still had a good bit in common. Dutch loved fossils and geographical history, and Andrew loved geology.

They'd always kept their connection secret, not wanting to raise attention to their plans for the oil field. It was too bad about Andrew, he thought, he was a good kid and didn't deserve to die so young.

Dutch was nudged out of his reverie by the distant sound of an approaching Model A. The engine was unmistakable. Some roughneck heading to the fields he thought. He put it out of his mind and went back to studying the papers. Andrew had been going to tell him something important, and was going to meet Dutch that very night he was killed.

They'd talked on the phone early that morning, Dutch recalled, and Andrew mentioned that he had finally solved the riddle, that he had the answers they were looking for. Andrew had asked Dutch to meet him out at his ranch that evening for dinner. He'd told him he could lay it all out for him at that time. That meeting never happened. Somehow Andrew was lured to the Riggins, a place he'd never had a mind to set a foot in, and in that moment had had his life stripped away. Such a shame.

His bride Heather was a beautiful and elegant southern gal. Walked and talked with grace. Dutch had attended their wedding back east and remembered spending time with her and Andrew at the big McCracken estate. A tragic death, murder no doubt. McMann was getting close. He and McMann never met in public, in fact they would only meet out of town. McCracken was very clear about that. Dutch and McMann had been meeting once a week comparing notes. McMann believed the killer of Andrew was close to being exposed. McCracken wanted there to be no doubt. McMann was to get the right man. That man would pay, of that Dutch was sure.

Suddenly the door to Dutch's office burst open and in walked or stumbled Raymond Hicks. That he had been drinking was very apparent. Hicks had left his car out in the desert and walked in, not wanting to alert Dutch to his approach.

Hicks held his .44 Winchester aimed right at Dutch's heart. The distance was about 20 feet, for Dutch's office was rather large. Hicks was known to be a crack shot though, so Dutch was quickly adding up his odds. They didn't look good. He chose a friendly approach. "Why Hicks, so nice of you to come a-courtin' so late in the evening. Had you called ahead I would have saved you the trip. I'm already married."

"Hrumpf!" Hicks replied. "You ain't married, Henry. Ain't a bride this side of Delaware'd have the likes of you. I want them papers, Dutch, then I'm going to burn this place down. Now where are they?" Hicks had allowed himself to get worked up into a frenzy.

Dutch, as he started to rise out of his chair, replied, "What papers do you mean, Hicks? I got papers all over this joint." Dutch deliberately glanced over to his safe, drawing a bit of Hicks' attention as he did so. Hicks fell for it and smiled an evil crooked smile, showing his gold tooth.

"All right, Dutch, open up that safe up or I'll fill you full of lead!"

"Them's big words, Hicks. How you going to get that safe open if'n I'm dead?"

Dutch had a good point, Hicks thought. His pickled brain was thinking fast. He'd seen safes like this before. He'd robbed enough banks back in the days with Laughing Sam Carey who always had a way to get them open. Dynamite had worked in the past, but that would draw too much attention. There were no hostages to threaten. Hicks was thinking fast and coming up blank.

As Hicks was a doing his thinking, Dutch nonchalantly placed today's copy of *The Record* over the papers he'd been studying. The last thing he wanted was for Hicks to walk out of here with them papers. Dutch would die first, but that wasn't in his plan.

Dutch knew Hicks was an old outlaw, and that he'd killed more than one unarmed man was not a question. He wouldn't think twice about putting a hole in Dutch's chest and Dutch knew it.

"What makes you think I got those papers, Ray?" Dutch used Hicks' first name, in a friendly manner.

"You got 'em, Henry. I know'd it from the start. Now start a-movin' before I start a-shootin'." Hicks used his rifle to direct Dutch over to the safe. "You better start a spinnin' that dial, and spinnin' it fast."

Dutch looked up at Hicks with the best beaten look he could muster, then started shuffling over toward the safe. "Okay, Ray, you win," Dutch agreed as he was moved toward the safe. "I'm all in anyway. This here desert's gotten the best of me. I'm heading out. Got me a gal in Tulsa wants me to come a-courtin'. I got me a bit put away back east. All I want now is a place to light and set. This oil digging business has me plumb warn out."

"Quit yer gabbing, Henry, and start a walkin'," Hicks ordered angrily. "I ain't interested in where you think you're a-goin'. All I'm interested in is them papers you got hid away in that safe. Now start a-spinnin'." As Hicks yelled the last words, they came accompanied with a coughing frenzy which produced plenty of blood. Hicks pulled out a handkerchief, with his left hand, while keeping the right hand holding a bead on Dutch's heart.

Dutch stopped and turned to look at Hicks with concern in his eye. "You're not well, Ray. Why don't you have a seat here and I'll boil you up some tea?"

Hicks looked through bloodshot eyes and yelled, "I'm just fine, Henry. Start a movin'." He coughed another convulsive bout, wiping off more blood.

Whether by accident or on purpose Dutch didn't know, but Hicks suddenly fired off a round. The impact in the far wall was coupled with the wind that bore the bullet's speed as it narrowly missed Dutch's skull.

"Move!" Hicks yelled while feeding another round into the chamber. His patience was wearing thin and Dutch knew it. He walked over to the safe then fumbled with the dial just enough to keep Hicks aggravated. "Been meaning to have the smith out here Hicks, this here locks all buggered up. I'll get it though, just takes a minute."

Hicks thought Dutch's story was plausible as he'd had some trouble with his safe as of late. He'd have to get that smithy out to the ranch himself.

"Heard there was some trouble with Reynolds," Dutch commented as he turned the dial to the left finding the final number of the combination. "Heard he was shot up or something. Too bad. I always liked Jack."

Hicks knew that was a lie and yelled, "He wasn't shot up, some coward dude cut his...."

As Hicks was ranting, Dutch spun the wheel, as he pulled the door open, he reached for the Colt, a maneuver he had practiced to the split second. He grabbed the gun, fell to the floor and rolled into a kneeling position.

The maneuver took him about five feet from the safe. The plan worked. Hicks, caught off guard amid his rantin' and coughin', fired off his first shot right towards where Dutch had just been a split second earlier. The bullet found the open safe and disappeared into the stack of bills.

Dutch always kept a round in the chamber with the safety off. He fired three fast shots. They made a perfect circle around Hicks' left breast pocket. Hicks was thrown backwards with the impact, hitting the back wall. As he hit the table, which housed a variety of Dutch's fossils, several fell to the floor. Hicks sat against the wall stunned.

Blood was reddening his chest as well as bubbling out his mouth. His eyes were fixed on Dutch's. He was trying to say something. Dutch came close and put his ear close to Hicks' mouth. He could barely make out the words, but their meaning was clear: "Bury me on Boot Hill."

With that, all motion stopped. Hicks was dead. As Dutch stood and took in the scene, he had to find the irony in it. He wasn't happy about Hicks being dead, but there he lay amidst the various fossils of the very land Hicks had ravaged throughout these past many years. What struck Dutch the most was the fact that right there lying in Hicks' lap, right where it had fallen, was the skull of the saber-tooth tiger. How appropriate, Dutch thought. Two deadly but now extinct predators, they couldn't have been more alike.

Moving Forward

After a few minutes, I decided I was alone so I made my way to my rig. Checking my Colt, I saw I'd left my spent round in the chamber. Replacing it, I thought about the situation. I should get in touch with Mac, he could be of help. On second thought, I didn't want to be responsible for anyone else getting killed. No, I'll go it alone.

Heading out of town, I chose the back roads, wanting to keep my destination a secret if I could. My first goal was to find Lou. She knew something and I needed that something in my own head.

As I crept down California Avenue, I started thinking about that rifle shot. That was a big gun. The bullet nearly broke the kitchen cabinet apart. Who was it used those big guns? It sounded like a Spencer 56. That large caliber rifle was used to kill buffalo. Who did I know who had a gun like that? On a whim, I turned down 15th Street. About a block away, I pulled over and killed the engine. Grabbing my Colt, I stuffed it in my belt as I made my way down the street. Ducking from shadow to shadow, I moved as a ghost. When I got to his car, I paused before I reached out my hand and placed it on the hood. Sure enough it was warm. The car belonged to Frank Bloomberg, and he also owned a Spencer 56. He'd mentioned it before. I remembered him bragging about how his grandfather had ridden along with Buffalo Bill Cody. He'd said his grandpa had made a living clearing the plains of buffalo. He was pretty proud of it. Said he and Cody had killed over 4,000 bison before it was through. I didn't rightly believe the Cody story since Bloomberg was a big bag of wind and not to be trusted for anything he said.

I was never one to beat around the bush so I decided to take the bull by the horns. I knocked on his door. When it opened, Bloomberg looked like he'd seen a ghost.

"Alex," he proclaimed, as though he was surprised to see me standing at all.

"That's right, Bloomberg, you missed!"

Bloomberg looked confused and rocked a bit on his feet. "I don't know what you're talking about, McCoy. What do you want?"

"Who is it, dear?" That was Sally Bloomberg, Frank's wife. She came to the door in a night robe held tightly to her chest with clutched hands.

"Hello, Sally," I said. "Sorry to disturb you but your husband came by for a visit and must have just missed me. I thought he must have something important to say so I decided I'd better stop by."

"Oh, I see. Is that where you were off to, honey?" Sally said turning her attention to her husband. Bloomberg just stood there frozen, caught in the act, speechless.

"Won't you please come in?" Sally asked swinging the door open. Bloomberg snapped out of his daze and then erupted, "No, he ain't comin' in!" he shouted and slammed the door. But not before I noticed his Spenser 56 leaning against a chair.

Remembering Lou, I headed back to my rig. I'd deal with Bloomberg later. He was too much of a coward to make a move or do anything now. I smiled as I recalled the look on his face when I shot that rabbit out of a dead run. No, he would keep his distance. That his wife had made a fool of him, blowing his cover, was almost comical, if I hadn't almost been killed, that is.

Someone had to have paid Bloomberg as a hit man; he was too dumb to have a major hand in any of this. He was like a coyote waiting for the scraps left by the lion. He'd probably just leave town now, leave his wife and all. The coward had no staying power. He'd played his hand and came up with deuces. He was out.

Heading back toward the 198, I contemplated my next move. There were a lot of loose ends here. I was thinking they would all be tied up in the next few days. I was right.

McCracken Makes Good

I found Lou in the shack by the train station. She was sitting at the little table with a small candle whose light gently danced around the room. She looked up when I came in and indicated the letter she was reading. "It come from Sadie, Alex. She's okay. Said a nice gentleman named Claude Bean had visited her and delivered my note to her. Seems Mr. McCracken made good on his word. Moved her to the desert somewhere. Sadie says there's a river runs close by with water as hot as to boil in some places. There are smaller pools that have a perfect temperature. Says she never seen the likes. Doctor Johnson, he knows Mr. McCracken, took her there. Called it a sanctuary," Lou said, tripping on the word being foreign to her. I thought she probably meant sanatorium. "Said I needed to come see her. She's feeling a bit better. Doc has her on quinine. Sadie said the doc called it the White Plague or tuberculosis. She takes laudanum, to ease the pain of coughing. She said her two sons have written her and want to visit her soon. She's afraid they won't come though, wanting to keep their kids healthy. I need to go to her, Alex. I'm afraid she doesn't have much time."

"Are you all right, Lou? Who do you suspect tore up your flat?" I asked.

"Yeah, I'm okay Alex. Whoever it was was an amateur, they missed the most obvious place." Lou put her hand down touching her carpetbag; it obviously contained all that she held dear. "I think whoever it was would have killed me though. I just get that feeling. I can't go back. I'll miss this town, Alex. It's the only home I know."

They were interrupted as the door to the shack swung open. Alex moved quickly to the side pulling his colt from his waist. McMann walk in and addressed the two. He glanced at the pistol in Alex's hand with only mild interest before he spoke.

"Raymond Hicks is dead," he began. "Apparently he consumed too much alcohol and decided to go try to bully Mr. Henry. Dutch wasn't for it, and shot Mr. Hicks right through the heart. It seems Mr. Henry was in possession of a high caliber pistol and knew how to use it. Anyway, I was on my way to visit Mr. Henry, but I found Sheriff Murray there looking over the scene. Raymond Hicks is dead all right. He was sitting there amongst the rest of the fossils in Dutch Henry's collection. I must say it was quite an exhibit."

The room was silent for a moment, it seems we were all taking the information in. Hicks was the big player in town. His death would create a vacuum, which would likely draw some lesser and maybe covert operatives out into the open. Hicks had stepped on a lot of toes, there would be plenty of turtles coming out of their shells.

Lou looked up at me and said, "I ain't a gonna miss Hicks. I know'd him a long time, but always felt like I was sleeping with a sidewinder. He'd talk to me about all the deals he'd made with the devil. I guess he's got to be cashin' in those chips with him right now."

After a moment, McMann spoke again, "There is more you should know. Jack Reynolds is dead as well, seemed to just slip away. Apparently he never did regain consciousness. Rex said he spied Darwin Anthony down at the Riggins, and that he'd been hitting the bottle pretty hard, drowning his sorrows I'd guess. I didn't take Mr. Anthony for a drinking man."

"He ain't," Lou replied. "Reynolds was the only friend he'd got. They rode into town together as two broken kids back in '06. Darwin never had no other friend I know'd of. He's likely to go off like a cannon. I'd stay clear. He'll be looking for the man 'cut off Reynolds finger." Lou paused for a minute then looked up at McMann, "Does Darwin know about Hicks yet?"

"Word hadn't arrived about the Hicks shooting when I last spoke to Rex, but I'm pretty sure the town would know by now," McMann commented.

I figure Darwin would have a rough time losing both Reynolds and Hicks in the same day. That's a lot to take for anyone.

"Thanks for lookin' after Sadie for me, Mr. McMann."

"You can thank Mr. McCracken for that, Lou, it was his doing," McMann told her.

"All the same, Mr. McMann, I appreciate it."

McMann grunted a response as he walked to the table and pulled up the third chair.

"She done wrote and told me about the place in the desert, the hot sulfur baths and that nice Mr. Bean who's been looking after her."

I could see an almost imperceivable stop in McMann's actions. It was Bean, that man was poison and I'd known it from the minute I'd laid eyes on him. "Bean's still there?" McMann demanded. His temper was not restrained as he asked.

Lou looked up a bit alarmed. "That's what she mentioned in the letter, Mr. McMann. Why? Is my sister in danger?"

McMann was silent for a moment looking at nothing in particular then responded. "No, she'll be fine. I'll take care of Bean."

I believed he would.

The Resolution

"What information do you have for me, Miss Williams?" McMann started. Then as an after-thought, almost under his breath, he said, "I think it's time to wrap this whole affair up. This desert has been terribly unfriendly to me, and my hives have not let up. I am needed back in Washington and to be quite honest, I am looking forward to a change in climate."

"The man you are looking for, Mr. McMann, is named Frank Bloomberg. He was there at the Riggins the night Andrew was killed. In fact, I just found out for certain that he'd done the killing."

"That's a big statement, Lou," I said, but somehow I was not surprised. "How can you be sure?"

"Peggy told me. She said he was all liquored up the other night when he come a courtin' her, and after some more drinking and a-rollin' around in the sheets, he started bragging. Peggy said he was a-talkin' big about becoming a silent partner with Hicks and all. Said he'd met privately with Hicks and that he paid him to clean up a few loose ends in town. He wanted

Peg to run away with him, said he'd leave his wife and everything."

Lou stopped talking and we sat in silence for a long moment.

"I believe I was one of those loose ends myself," I said quietly. McMann looked at me expectantly but said nothing. I went ahead and explained the attempt on my life that very night and my visit to Bloomberg's house. I mentioned how his wife, Sally, blew his cover and how I saw the buffalo gun sitting against the chair. I also mentioned the warning Bloomberg had given me a couple weeks back on our would-be fishing trip.

McMann pushed his chair back and stood. "You'd better take Lou somewhere safe Mr. McCoy. I'll be wrapping things up here soon and then heading home. I appreciate both of your cooperation in this affair, as does Mr. McCracken."

Turning to Lou he pulled an envelope out of his pocket and handed it to her. "This is everything you will need. Good luck, Miss Williams."

With that McMann turned and walked out of our lives.

Cleaning House

Darwin awoke the next day in his own bed. How he got there he had no idea. He assumed that a couple of the roughnecks in Hicks' employ guided him home. As he walked to the eating room he was faced with the events of yesterday. Not only had Reynolds died in his arms, but now he heard that his uncle went and got himself killed. The emptiness hit him all at once and he felt a deep pit of despair. For a brief moment he thought of his mom and almost missed her. Darwin had a hard time understanding his emotions. For the first time in many years he felt directionless.

Entering the eating area he came across Cookie, who just sat on his stool looking out the window which faced the old barn. Cookie had been an old man when Darwin ate his first bowl of chili some 15 years ago, but now he was ancient. He stooped over so far that his braided beard almost touched the floor. His back resembled that of a camel and his knees were wobbly as he walked.

Cookie turned his gaze to Darwin, "This no good, boss, Mr. Hicks good man, now he dead." After a minute Cookie realized Darwin was standing there and that he was slacking in his duties and tried to jump into action. His efforts fell short though and he simply fell back in his chair hitting his head on the solid oak table behind him. Darwin looked down with blank eyes as the dark red blood seeped into the cracks of the floor.

Suddenly he remembered that fateful day, back in '06. The quake had just hit, he ran outside leaving his ma lying buried under what was left of their little shack. He recalled hearing a man scream, a gunshot, then a dead man lying in front of him with blood soaking into the dry, sandy road. As he looked into the vacant eyes of what had been Cookie, he was also looking into the eyes of that dead man so many years ago.

Time seemed to have collapsed. There he was, a boy all of 14, he had his life ahead of him. What about the choices he had made? What was the worth of a man? His father lay buried in a foreign land, his uncle would soon be buried on Boot Hill along with his best friend. His mother never said she loved him or goodbye. And his horse, Willy, died an old swayback nag, forgotten and alone. He thought of his life. He was nothing, had always been nothing, and even now accounted for nothing.

As he walked out on the porch of the old ranch house, he saw Old Judd, sitting under an oak tree, smoking what Darwin knew would be a hand-rolled smoke.

What of Judd? Darwin wondered. He never really liked him much anyway. He was always bossin' Darwin around and never had no give in him. Who did he think he was ordering him around all the time? His uncle was the only one who should tell him what to do.

As Darwin sat on the porch watching Judd sit in his old rocker smoking that cigarette, he felt a spark of life ignite somewhere deep inside him. He allowed that thought to burn into anger until he was about to burst into flames himself. Judd had to go! That was all there was to it. This ranch was his now, his uncle left it to him. He would kick Judd the hell off his property as soon as the dust settled.

"Judd," Darwin yelled, not quite up to his mind's idea of power. "I think you better come over here. Cookie had an accident, I think he's dead." Why couldn't he order Judd around the way he wanted to? Was he a coward? No matter; soon Judd be off the ranch any way.

Darwin watched as the lanky cowboy sauntered over to the ranch house. He was as bowlegged as they come, looking like he'd slept in the saddle. He was as skinny as a fence post. His skin resembled that of a fall apple that dried on the tree, and that hat that he wore, you could see clean through and it looked like it had been shot at a time or two.

When Judd looked down at Cookie all broke up, he took his hat off and holding it over his heart said some words under his breath, then placed it back on his head. Without looking at or saying a thing to Darwin he just picked Cookie up like he was a feather and carried him out toward what they called Boot Hill. It was up a gentle slope back of the barn. Darwin let his eyes follow and was astonished to see two other bodies up on the hill, wrapped in burlap. Those would have been the bodies of Hicks and Reynolds. What astounded Darwin even more, was the two piles of dirt depicting the graves Judd had dug that morning. Maybe this was what Darwin resented about Judd. He just got things done. He never had to be asked; he just know'd what to do. Hicks was always hounding Darwin and telling him what to do. Darwin hated that. Judd never had the same treatment from Hicks. Well, good riddance. Soon Judd would be off his ranch, that was that.

In fact, why wait? Darwin decided to go into town, find Hicks' attorney, Bates, and then go over to see Judge Lindsey. He'd get the deed transferred to his name, legal, and then kick Judd the hell off of the place. He'd give him an old horse and send him over the hill. With satisfaction in his eye, he jumped into his rig and headed to town.

<u>*Ma and Lou*</u>

When I pulled up to the old ranch, it was about two in the morning. Lou was asleep in the seat next to me, I could tell from the snoring. Ma was awake as I knew she would be. She was setting there by the small fire rocking in her chair. She was older now and didn't do much getting around. She loved to just look into the fire and imagine what those flames were saying. She would dream about Pa and me in the old days. She said she was happy though, she just loved that she even knew Pa at all.

When I introduced Lou to Ma, there was an immediate kinship. They were both from the Midwest and as I watched Lou talk to Ma, I could see them both begin to take on a new strength. It amazed me to see Lou out of the Fifth Street environment. One would never suspect her of her past. Knowing they were both in good hands, I said my goodbyes and headed back to town. There was too much at stake and too much going on for me to stay away.

The Answer, Hanging on the Shed

I was heading up the grade that lead from the train depot to Coalinga when I saw up in the distance the lights of Murray's patrol car as well as that of his other deputy, Flannery. As I approached I pulled to a stop. There was a crowd of people formed around a small barn by what was the border of the Hicks/Henry southern boundary. This was a spot of much contention. Hicks and Dutch had been fighting over the rights to drill there for some time.

As I got out of my rig, I noticed Mac was there as well as Mayor Adams. When Mac saw me he beckoned me over. He said they'd all gotten an anonymous call to get out to this spot quickly. Mac said that when he got here, Flannery was already here, and Murray arrived just after. Mayor Adams arrived five minutes later.

When I asked Murray what it was all about, he pointed to something I hadn't noticed on arrival. There, nailed to the side of the barn was a fresh corpse. Bloomberg had been nailed up there as if crucified, and hanging around his neck was a piece of paper written on with ink. As I approached what was once Bloomberg, I could read the message. "I KILLED ANDREW" was all it said. As my gaze was drawn to Bloomberg's right hand, I saw the bloody stump where his index finger had once been. I could fill in the rest. I was sure that there was an early model Packard heading east. In that car behind the wheel was a big man, and in the back seat a very small well-dressed gentleman awaiting relief from a hives breakout. That Murray would not be in pursuit was an obvious conclusion.

My bed never felt so good. It was about ten in the morning when I finally awoke. As I went to the kitchen, I was confronted with the splintered mess of what was once my cabinet door. Beth would be fit to be tied when she got home. I whipped up some grub and then jumped into my rig and headed to *The Record*. I had a lot of writing to do and wanted to get right on it.

As I pulled up to the front of the building, I saw two very large well-dressed men talking to Mac. They weren't as big as Rex but were definitely cut from the same cloth.

As I parked and got out of my rig, all eyes met mine.

"Alex," Mac said, "I want to introduce you to Vinni and Tony Zambino. They have come from back east and want to have a word with Sheriff Murray and his deputy. Do you have any idea of their whereabouts?"

I could see the twinkle in Mac's eye, him knowing as well as I that the sheriff and the deputy would be high-tailing it for the hills, looking for any unoccupied skunk hole to stick their heads in.

The Public Reading

I was sitting at my desk trying to put together all the details of the last week when Dutch Henry walked in.

"Howdy, Alex," he offered. "I see you are hard at work. Looks like journalism ain't all that easy these days."

"You're speaking the truth, Dutch. What can I do for you?"

"I got a note from Judge Lindsey regarding Raymond Hicks' estate. Apparently he feels it's important that this reading be public. I guess with all of the shenanigans these last few years, he wants to make a clean sweep of the underhanded thievery associated with Hicks and his estate. He mentioned in his note to me that I should invite you. He thinks the citizens of Coalinga should be privy to the outcome."

"Sounds like something I shouldn't miss, Dutch. When does this all take place?"

"3:00 today, Alex. He wants to put an end to it right now."

I grabbed my notebook and followed Dutch out the door.

Bailiff William Mitchell said, "All rise," as Judge Harold Lindsey entered the courtroom. As he slammed the gavel down on the sounding block, the room grew quiet.

"Today is the day we will settle the affairs and estate of the late Raymond Hicks. I understand we have in this court his last will and testament as provided by his attorney, Mr. Bates."

Lindsey turned his attention to Bates and addressed him directly. "Mr. Bates do you solemnly swear that the documents provided to the court are those of the last known wishes of one Raymond Hicks?"

"Yes, your honor, those are the last papers Mr. Hicks left in my possession regarding any distribution of his holdings in the event of his untimely death."

"Bailiff, would you please retrieve the papers and approach the bench?"

Without speaking Mitchell carried out the order. "Let it be noted that the envelope has been delivered with an unbroken wax seal bearing the initials RH. It is also dated June 30th, 1918."

There were murmurs throughout the courtroom as ordinary folks were interested to hear the outcome of the event. That Darwin Anthony would be named the heir of the majority of his fortune was taken for granted, but Hicks had a lot of irons in the fire, and likely had many dealings with members of the community who were no doubt promised much.

Lindsey tore open the envelope containing the documents. There was a deadly silence in the crowd as he pulled the papers free. You could feel the anticipation in the room as he began to read the documents.

"You can be sure by the reading of this, my last will and testament, that I am resting comfortably in my new home on Boot Hill. I can only hope that this reading is taking place around the year 1940; this would mean that I lived to be a rich old man. If this is not the case, then my schemes fell short of their mark. Let it be known that I am proud of my life, be it what it may have been. I crawled out of the mud and made a place for myself in this world. The lust for the Black Gold found in the Coalinga hills provided for me a reason to live. I believe that in a sobering moment I can say I have gone mad for the want of it. Yet so be it and so did I move forward on my plan to be the Baron of the Coalinga oil fields. I believe that Mr. Rockefeller's questionable actions back east have far exceeded any harm I have done in pursuing my dream.

"Today I wish to dispose of all of my holdings in the following manner:

First, I would like to donate the section of land that I hold southeast of California Street to the Coalinga

School District. I would like to see the children of this town be provided with an education second to none."

There was a startled rumble amongst the crowd. That Hicks would do such a thing was not only a surprise, but unthinkable.

"Second, I would like to leave my holdings in the Maritime Canneries on Monterey's Cannery Row to Penelope Barnes, granddaughter to Judd Barnes."

There was again a murmur in the court. Mostly because no one knew that Hicks' involvement in the cannery existed, but secondly because most people didn't even know about Judd or of his granddaughter.

Judge Lindsey continued on down the list of smaller items, including leaving a stipend to Cookie. Deeding him a place on the farm to live out his days.

What was surprising was the home in Monterey he left to the Lady known as Lou, along with $50,000 in a bank account. This created an uproar in the crowd and Judge Lindsey almost broke his gavel bringing the court to order.

Finally the judge came to the final distribution of the Hicks holdings. I looked over to Darwin who was stirring in his seat but looking on with a bit of smug contempt.

"As to the twenty thousand acres which make up the Double Bar 7, as well as all the 3,000 plus head of cattle, all of the out buildings and the ranch house itself, I leave all ownership and possessions in the capable hands of my lifelong friend and partner, Judd Barnes."

There was an uproar in the courtroom which went on for at least five minutes. Darwin sat stunned in his seat.

Judge Lindsey continued, "The vast holdings of the Hicks oil company I leave to Judd Barnes and his granddaughter Penelope Barnes." There was still an amazing amount of noise coming from the crowd.

"To my nephew who I raised and trusted with my life, I leave the sum of one hundred dollars. Having trusted you with my life, I have lived to see the deceit and dishonesty of a con man. You have stolen from me and purchased property behind my back, for this I have no sympathy or forgiveness. You arrived at my ranch on an old beat down horse. Not only did you abandon this horse in short order, but you left him to die in his stable. Take this hundred dollars I leave you, buy yourself another horse and ride out of town. You have more of your good-for-nothing father in you than I suspected.

"To the Citizens of Coalinga I leave an account in the bank containing $50,000. Please use this to improve the water quality. It stinks!"

With that, Judge Lindsey stood followed by the blasting voice of William Mitchell, "All Rise!"

There was a cacophony of voices echoing down the halls of the courthouse as the stunned citizens poured into the streets.

Darwin remained seated in the courthouse. Nobody noticed when he left, and no one cared.

I was off to *The Record* to prepare the morning addition of "It Happened on Fifth Street".

Coalinga had come of age. The riffraff had gone and the citizens united, seeing to it that Coalinga would never again fall into the hands of greed. It was the dawning of a new year, a new time. Coalinga spent the money Hicks left them to clean up the town. They built a new school, cleaned up the water, and much to the surprise of the world, declared itself a dry city. With the banning of liquor and the ousting of the shady ladies and unsavory businessmen, Coaling Station A was settling down, on its way to fading into history.

The morning sun arose early casting its golden rays across the stark desert skies. The reddish gables and ancient cathedrals scraped the horizon as the cool morning breeze spoke of the heat of the day yet to come. There was a distinctly different feel to the air this morning, empty of the gentle moisture of the once-familiar valley, but steeped with the wild smell of cactus flowers.

Lou walked out the door of the abode she had quickly grown accustomed to. Sadie sat in a rocker enjoying the morning air. "Mother would have loved it here," Sadie remarked.

Lou clutched the Clan's brooch that was her mother's to her chest and replied, "I wish I could have told her I loved her and said goodbye."

The Row Laid Low

Coalinga June 1930

This is Mac's rendition of the fire, which flattened Whisky Row aka Fifth Street in the terrible fire of 1915. The Lady known as Lou in 'Coaling Station A' is characterized after the famous Fifth Street inhabitant, The Lady Known as Jean.

Whiskey Row has been laid low,
By a fire of unknown cause.
This tale is told of a hero bold,
One of the city's laws.

He happened to be on his bet at three
When the fire first broke out.
The sleeping heads all left their beds
 When they heard his warning shout!

He spread the news 'mid the smoke and the booze
Along the famous row.
How they swarmed from their hives in the Whiskey dives
Was anything but slow.

But one poor dame in her life of shame
Failed to hear his call.
She was still in there 'mid the smoke and the flare
When the house began to fall!

Walt faced the crowd and shouted loud,

Giving a curt salute;
"Is there none who dares to climb the stairs
And rescue a prostitute!

They all looked scared and no one dared!
Then Walt turned toward the dive,
And dashed inside and the people cried
"You'll never come out alive!"

Ten minutes passed when Walt at last
Came staggering out the door;
Safe in the charms of his manly arms
He held a naked Whore.

This is the naked truth of the case,
When out of the smoky screen,
The flames he braved and the life he saved
Was a lady that's known as Jean.

I sing the praise of this guy named Hayes,
He's the hero of the day.
In his official duty he saved his booty,
Let's raise the blighter's pay!

Buenas noches.
F. J. 'Mac' McCollum
aka Joe King, 1930

My grandpa, around age 77, with a 39-inch Dolly Vardin trout he caught at Huntington Lake (circa 1960).

Fay James "Mac" McCollum
(aka Joe King)
1883 - 1980

About the Author

Duncan McDougall McCollum was born the youngest child of early California pioneer descendants. From them, he developed rich historical stories based on their pioneer experiences.

His father's family made the trek across the Great Plains to California around 1849, traveling with a wagon train. His great-great grandfather, James McDougall, once a constable in Scotland, traveled to America after he was reprimanded for arresting an English nobleman for a legal infraction.

Embarrassed and insulted by the injustice, he told his wife, "Beth, I'm moving to the New Country."

"That's fine Jamie, but you're taking our eldest son with ya'." Jamie and his son were soon on a ship bound for America. After three days at sea, young Jamie Jr. came out of hiding as a stowaway and was immediately taken in by the captain. His pa had warned him not to let on they were related. Once on land, Jamie grabbed his boy and made a run for it.

James McDougall settled in Salinas around 1850 and became the first town marshal, as well as other things. Duncan's grandfather was born in 1883 and died at the early age of 97, but not before he passed on his yarns and limericks to him.

From his mother's family, Duncan recalls sitting around his Grandma Sudie's kitchen table listening to his Uncle Bill Orton and his older sisters recant the stories of early California. Sula May, known as "Sudie", was born in 1892 lived to be 82. Duncan always loved to hear them talk about the early days of their parents pioneering the great Central Valley.

The Orton family arrived in America somewhere around 1634. They were part of the early pioneers who settled what is now Connecticut and fought off the very dangerous and brutal Pequot Indians, establishing one of the earliest settlements in the region. His great-great grandfather, Julius Orton, had joined the cavalry and was deployed to the Nevada Territory to fight the Mexican Army culminating in a United States victory, ending the Mexican-American War. The year was 1848, and Julius found himself in Nevada when gold was discovered in Sutter's Mill in California. He ended up striking it rich in Hang Town, better known now as Placerville. Wisely, he contacted his brother Silas and talked him into coming to California to stand guard while he mined his claim. Without someone to watch his back, a gold miner's life span was very short.

All of these rich stories shaped Duncan's life and he is

very happy to share them with you now.

Dr. Duncan McCollum, a practicing chiropractor, the acorn that never fell far from the family tree, he has raised his family of three kids, Will, Natalie and Angus in Aptos, California, with his beautiful wife Elizabeth.

SETON
PUBLISHING

68467349R00129

Made in the USA
San Bernardino, CA
04 February 2018